Thermoil

Selected Shorts by a Romantic Engineer

Kevin Sheehan

North
Country
Press

ISBN 978-1-943424-17-7

Library of Congress Control Number: 2016961640

"Aquaplaning on Sebago" and "Charley Watkins" are reprinted with minor changes from *Down East*. "Wurlitzer's Military Band" is reprinted from the *Bulletin* of the Musical Box Society International. "Zat So?" is reprinted with minor changes from *Out of the Cradle*.

Front cover photo of Thermoil engine by Aumann Auctions, Inc. Back cover photo and Robert photo on page 130 by Linda Wright Sheehan.

North Country Press
Unity, Maine

FOR FOREST

Table of Contents

A Two-Stroke Affair

In 1956 I was a spindly and crater-faced nineteen, driven by subterranean secretions to win the hand of Linda Wright from Hartsdale, New York, whom I had met the previous October at Cornell. She was, thankfully, somewhat better padded than I, and her complexion was clear, if on the saffron side. Black and purple looked good on her. By any standard her legs were exquisite, and I found her long oval face framed by long dark hair irresistible.

I'd made little headway during our freshman year, Linda having affirmed her independence while lying with her head in my lap on the couch in Willard Straight Hall's east lounge just before Christmas and again in May while traversing the quad at my side under a full moon, lugging a blanket concealed in her typewriter case. Not until I picked her up one steamy Wednesday evening in July in a sanguine Messerschmitt Kabinenroller 200 did she reconsider.

* * * * * *

William Ashbury Wright, corporation attorney and Linda's father, is hovering above the Messerschmitt's bubble canopy before I can switch off.

"Uh...Kevin. Would you mind parking a little farther from the house? Your exhaust is...uh...asphyxiating the rhododendrons."

I unwind the key, and the Fichtel & Sachs one-lunger in the rear stops pinging rings of blue smoke at the leathery leaves shrouding Bill's immaculate half-timber house and slowly fut-futs to a stop.

"What do you think of her, sir?"

Before the deliberate gentleman, who is old enough to be her grandfather, can reply, Linda's face appears opposite his, bloated by the optical distortion in the transparent Plexiglas dome. She's scowling. (It had taken her more than a few outings in my 1929 Ford to stop squirming with embarrassment beside me, so I was

1

expecting her discomfort.) Interrupting her father, she bends low and bellows in my right ear through the open sliding sash.

"You expect me to ride in *this*?"

She's breathing on my neck and peering in at the passenger seat behind me, a skimpy red Naugahyde pad barely wide enough to accommodate her slender hips. Instinctively, I restrike the lifesaving pose I'd acquired in order to avoid inadvertent lane changes on the Hutch: elbows braced on both open window sills, hands visegripping the drooped horns of the creamy plastic handlebar that rotated before me a mere sixty degrees from lock to lock. Then I realize where I am and reach for the latch, turn it and begin lifting the bubble canopy.

"What's wrong with riding in the back?" I ask.

"For one thing, I get sick."

Linda moves to stand next to her father at my left, to avoid being bumped by the hinged canopy rolling over into the curbside lane where it dangles, supported by a single leather thong. I push off with my feet, and the driver's seat obligingly rises and moves back on its four-bar linkage, tracing an arched path, providing room to extricate my long legs from under the dash. Stepping over the high, v-shaped sill and lowering the driver's seat, I gesture for Linda to enter.

"For another, we have to pick up Charlene. Remember?"

She makes no move to enter but stands with arms akimbo, glaring. I look down at the tiny tandem cockpit and feel my ears getting warm. I try again.

"Playland's only a fifteen-minute ride from her house. You can sit on her lap."

Ignoring me, Linda slowly begins circling the tricycle scooter, scrutinizing it with eyes narrowed to slits, brow furrowed with disapproval.

"It looks like the aborted offspring of a Hoover that mated with a praying mantis."

"It's safe as a church," I lie. "Besides, you rode on the back of Ivan's Vespa, and that's ten times more dangerous than this."

Fortunately, Bill doesn't know what a Vespa is. His mind is on a personal problem in the garage, and he collars me.

"Kevin...uh...I'd like you to assist me with something on my Buick."

I follow him, partly out of deference but mostly to duck Linda's next salvo, delivered close over my left shoulder.

"You think I'll go anywhere with you, in any contraption that suits your fancy, don't you?"

I didn't have to say a word in my defense. From the doorway, Bill booms, "Now, Linda. Uh...I'm trying to engage Kevin in a matter here. Have a sense of...uh...uh...of decency."

Whether it was surprise at her father's early acceptance of a suitor or fear of his delayed reprimand (most likely delivered at breakfast the next morning after he'd had a full night to ruminate), I'll never know. For whatever reason, Linda retreats, and when I return to the Kabinenroller after showing Bill how to set stations on his Buick's pushbutton radio, I find her perched, rigid with resignation in the rear seat. I pull up the helm seat, hop in and drop to the controls. Pushing in the key before twisting it sets a red jewel glowing as the Dynastart cranks the ten-horsepower single backwards, accompanied by a quavering murmur soon punctuated by desultory pings. I pull the canopy over our heads, latch it and yank the shifter up into low before glancing in the mirror.

Linda is scrunched so far down in the seat that I see only her black and white polka-dotted hair bow projecting above her head like a helicopter rotor. I ease in the clutch and back down the driveway and out onto Caterson Terrace. Bill is grinning a deep vee, but his smile quickly fades when I kill the ignition in the middle of the street, wait for the engine to stop and crank it ahead by twisting the key without pressing it in, lighting the green jewel that indicates forward rotation. The erratic popping and jiggling resumes and, without touching the shifter, I launch the rolling crustacean, leaving Bill standing at the end of his driveway, enveloped in a blue haze. I declutch and jab the progressive shifter down into second, decisively, to avoid fetching neutral and evoking an impotent scream from the engine compartment. We're barely out of Bill's sight when Linda's bituminous eyes appear larger than life-size in the mirror.

"You think this is funny, don't you?" Her saliva is spraying the back of my neck. "Don't you *ever* do this to me again."

She shoves my right shoulder at the word 'ever,' and the Messerschmitt darts into the left lane. I yank it back just in time to avoid an oncoming Cadillac.

"And don't you ever do *that* again."

"What? This?"

I twitch the handlebar and the scooter zig-zags alarmingly. Linda burps.

"You'll have my supper down your neck if you don't cut that out."

I pull over to the curb and gingerly brake to a stop. Linda is white and swallowing hard. I feel my heart begin to pound. It's happening to me again: I'm trapped in a confined space with someone about to throw up.

"Okay," I say, starting to tremble, "You've made your point. Now, take some deep breaths, and the nausea will pass."

I hear her heave several puffs and see in the mirror that the color is returning to her cheeks. Greatly relieved, I sigh and slide lower in my seat. A minute goes by in silence before she works up enough saliva to clatter in a small voice, talking to the floor directly in front of her.

"I'm an only child, separated by not one but two generations from my parents. Their values, their principles—oh, God, their *principles*—are from another century. I didn't want to have to tell you but, each time you leave, Daddy asks me why your shoes aren't shined and why you're not wearing a tie. After dinner, Mom whines about the way you jounce your leg and jiggle the table so. Later, I hear Daddy complain about having to refinish the rung on the chair you occupied. And now I'm going to have to listen to another of his lectures about 'sensible' driving and how teenagers—he'll never mention names—are taking foolish risks and shouldn't be given a license until age twenty-one. Are you beginning to see what I'm up against?"

She lifts her head and seizes a hank of hair above each breast and pulls, which draws the corners of her already steeply inclined eyelids down further.

"P-l-e-a-s-e don't do this to me."

* * * * * *

My two-stroke affair had originated at the end of June. I was early to meet my father, arriving on the 6:04 from Manhattan. To kill time, I looked over the exotic machinery in the New Canaan, Connecticut, commuter lot. There, dwarfed by the Mercedes and Bentley that flanked it, was the most peculiar little car I'd ever laid eyes on. I could hardly call it a car. It had only three wheels, none bigger than a motor scooter's, two in front under clam shell fenders, and one in the back, where I deduced the engine resided, judging from the louvers and the oily stub of an exhaust pipe poking out from under the rear valance. The whole contraption was maybe nine feet long, four feet wide and four feet high. I could see through the narrow, transparent canopy that its two seats were disposed one ahead of the other, like in a fighter cockpit. There was no steering wheel, just a handlebar—and only one windshield wiper. Its two headlights were about a foot and a half apart, giving it the appearance of an approaching PB-Y Catalina. I could see no mark of identification except a medallion on its nose that looked like a hovering hummingbird set in a circle of polished aluminum.

Curiosity overpowered my sense of propriety and, with only moments to spare before the train arrived, I hastily scribbled a note to the car's owner on a scrap of paper and slipped it under the wiper blade.

> Pardon the intrusion, but I am very interested in your car and would like to know more about it. Would you be so kind as to call me at your convenience. My number is Woodward 6-9283.
>
> Sincerely,
> Kevin Sheehan
> The Barn, Sunset Hill Road
> New Canaan, Connecticut

To my great surprise and joy, two days later as I was finishing supper, the owner called, a Mr. Arthur Kittredge Watson, who lived only a half mile from me on the corner of Weed and Elm. (I learned later, much to my embarrassment, that Mr. Watson was then president of IBM World Trade Corporation.) Would I like to drive it, he asked? I would, very much, I said, and thanked him for responding so quickly and courteously. I couldn't wait for the week to end.

True to his word, Mr. Watson met me at the back door and ushered me to the carriage house. On the way he explained that the car was just a toy to him; he'd acquired it to entertain himself on the way to and from the train station. (I never doubted his motives as I scanned the palatial surroundings of the stone-walled Watson compound.) Apparently the novelty had worn off because he immediately offered to loan me the car for the following week. I remember the lump in my throat as I gratefully accepted his offer. It seemed tragic that this distinguished gentleman had more money than he could enjoy.

I was working that summer as an engineer's assistant at Machlett Laboratories on Steamboat Road in Greenwich, and decided to put my popularity, which so far had been zero, to the test. Arriving just before the start of work on Monday, I wheeled into an empty spot in the middle of the employees lot in full view of the shop. I was surrounded before I could get the canopy open. Stony engineers fogged the Plexiglas with questions breathed close above, about the car's fuel consumption, stability and handling, while snickering secretaries stood at a safe distance, pointing as if they were viewing an adorable marmot at the zoo. For those few minutes I felt admired, envied perhaps, by my peers. And then it was down to business, and I receded in their minds to my former speck.

But I was determined not to be ignored by Miss Wright. While I had use of the Kabinenroller, I decided to deploy it as a decoy. After Linda's reaction to it on Wednesday, I was chary about using it for our Friday night date at Delmonico's. Although she had adjusted to riding shotgun, and even got to giggling on Charlene's lap when the attendant at Playland's parking lot asked if we were one of the amusement rides, her tentative parting kiss at the door that night told me that I was pushing my luck.

Nevertheless, I was persuaded—ordered would be more accurate—by my mother, to whom I'd made the mistake of telling about the Wright's distaste for my decorum, to not only use the Messerschmitt on Friday but to dress in Dad's tuxedo and stovepipe hat and bring flowers for her mother. From the tidbits of information I brought to the dinner table, Mom had been able to piece together a pretty good picture of Linda's parents, good enough to decide she didn't like them, and this tale was the clincher. She wanted to retaliate.

Reluctantly, I put on Dad's monkey suit that had been stored in our attic since their wedding in 1935. Mom polished a silver mint tray and a dime for the Greenwich toll attendant on the Merritt Parkway. I was to place the dime on a crocheted doily atop the tray and proffer it to Dad's toll collector friend Mr. Tanner, who would be on duty that evening. When I got to the Wrights', I was to approach the door with the bouquet behind my back and, when Linda's mother Eva opened the door, bow low and say, "Good evening, Mrs. Wright," present the flowers and add, "Something to brighten your table. Is your lovely daughter at home?"

So prompted, I left The Barn for Hartsdale.

* * * * * *

The KR-200 fires quickly, eager to participate in our prank. Soon the stars are streaming overhead between the pines lining the Merritt. From the rear, the cooling fan wails a sinusoidal song as the hills are crested one by one and put behind.

The toll booth lights appear ahead, and I fumble the tray, losing the dime under the seat. The Kabinenroller darts like a bat hunting mayflies as I grope for the coin and replace it on the doily. I get the vehicle under control just in time to stuff it into the booth. Mr. Tanner holds out his hand. For a split second I lose my nerve and almost give myself away.

"Hello, sir. Lovely evening."

7

He's about to answer when I see his ruddy face lose color and crease with shock as I present the tray with my white-gloved hand. His stubby fingers scrabble about the tray, trying to swipe the glistening dime. He finally manages to drag it to the edge of the tray and get a grip on it. I'm trying to suppress an explosion of laughter; its potential is making my hand shake, and I dare not look at him directly. The scene in my mirror as I pull away will hang in my mind's gallery forever. Ignoring the car following me, Tanner is leaning from his waist out of the booth, mouth agape, rubbing his eyes and squinting in the floodlight, straining to fathom the receding apparition.

I'd heard a rumor that three-wheeled vehicles were going to be banned from the Hutch because of their tendency to go out of control and overturn, so I braced extra hard for the sharp turns and narrow lanes and once more managed to confine the tiny corn-popper's weaving to its own lane. Joints in the concrete pavement were a more treacherous obstacle; you couldn't prepare for them. In the turns, the thing would hop sideways when it struck the gap. I learned to stay well inside when entering turns, to allow for the inevitable drift. If the turn was a long one, I'd try to recover my inside line midway by twitching the handlebar slightly between hops.

In order to surprise the Wrights, I switch off early, coast down Caterson Terrace, and park at the foot of the driveway. I get out and steal to the back door unnoticed, and ring the bell. Lucky for me, Eva opens the door. She sways a moment before speaking.

"Good evening," I say, bowing low as instructed.

"Hello, Kevin. Don't you look nice?"

I straighten and present the roses that are already limp from being parched by the jet of engine cooling air uncontrollably emanating from the heater hose that dangles from the right sill.

Incredibly, I hear myself say, "Something to brighten your table. Is your lov—?"

"Bill! Bill, come quick! Kevin's here and he's dressed in tails."

Linda appears behind her mother. Eva turns to her.

"Isn't he adorable? He's all gussied up. Bill." Then, almost in a whisper, "You don't suppose Kevin knows about—?"

Linda pushes past her mother and grasps my arm firmly. "Don't bother Dad. He's busy in the study." I feel her grip strengthen as she tugs me forcibly toward the car.

"Bill."

"Bye, Mom. I'll be home by eleven."

Linda's parting words to her mother are delivered over her shoulder through clenched teeth as she scolds me with her eyes and tows me down the driveway. This time I don't have to coax her into the Messerschmitt. I think she would have mounted a camel if that's what I'd provided for our transport. Releasing her hold on my arm, she throws open the canopy and steps into the back, flops down, folds her arms across her chest and waits, hissing quietly, for me to enter.

I could see this was going to be my last date with the brooding siren I'd selected to be my wife. (At that age, it seemed a short step between falling in love and the altar, but I had the good sense not to breathe a word of my intentions to Miss Wright until I was sure the feeling was mutual.) Without looking at her, I get us underway, slipping the clutch to launch the KR smoothly. Hearing no burp from behind, I take the risk of opening with an explanation of my appearance.

"This is all Mom's fault. She insisted I don this ridiculous penguin outfit to impress your folks. Can you believe it?"

I glance in the mirror. Linda is staring at the mint tray on the floor. When I finish, she looks up into the mirror. Her pupils resemble anthracite cinders. Beneath her long winter nose, her mouth is pursed to a dot.

"No."

"I'm not kidding. Do you think I like wearing this foppery?"

No answer from the back seat.

"Look, this has been hard on me, too. My mother hates social amenities. She wouldn't even come to my graduation."

"And I suppose she won't come to our wedding."

"What did you say?" I ask incredulously, moving closer to the mirror.

Louder from the back seat: "I said, I suppose your mother won't come to our wedding, either."

Linda is sitting defiantly erect. Her hair, parted in the middle, is symmetrically streaming from the windows on both sides of the narrow canopy like the wings of a raven in flight. She's speaking in a deep and controlled tone that makes my insides crawl with desire.

We're only a couple blocks from the restaurant. I force myself to keep driving, not wanting to exhibit premature ecstasy and possibly smother the fragile spark I think I detect.

"Almost there," I say, pretending my mind is on our dinner engagement.

* * * * * *

I returned the Messerschmitt that Sunday. Linda and I got married three years later, on June 20, 1959. It was a lavish social affair. My mother did not attend.

Aquaplaning on Sebago

My grandfather had wanted a son. He was demonstrative in his disappointment, and my mother spent her youth trying to win his acceptance. In an effort to please, she earned her way from lowly Water Witch to regal Gypsy Queen at Camp Wohelo on Sebago Lake in Raymond, Maine, and she dedicated herself to learning all that she could about the ways of the water and the woods. Little wonder she chose me, her first son, to fill the frame she could not.

During the forties and fifties, my family summered on an island at the north end of Sebago's Jordan Bay. It was there that Mom taught me how to prime a pump, make fire by friction and ice cream by crank, swim the breaststroke for miles—"Up, out, and together hard!"—and propel a canoe in absolute silence, Cree-style, by feathering the paddle under water.

As a young boy, during infrequent breaks from my camp chores and Mom's rigorous training, I'd slip down to the dock and watch the motorboats howl past the rock breakwater and sputter into Turtle Cove. With a thirteen-year-old boy's intrinsic envy of speed, I longed to have a motor to clamp on the transom of our square-stern Rangeley rowboat.

There were also practical reasons. We had to ferry ourselves and our supplies to our island camp, a half mile from the mainland, an arduous task that I thought would eventually convince Mom that we needed an outboard. But she remained adamant that we do things manually. By the summer of 1950, I had begun to despair. It looked like it was going to be yet another season of bulling our way around the lake.

And so it was with little enthusiasm that I approached my birthday that summer. I was accustomed to receiving from my mother a canoe paddle to decorate and varnish or a Swiss army knife. Dad habitually gave me a book for some light reading (usually a lengthy classic set in the Middle Ages). But this birthday was different. In addition to my gift from Mom—a machete, which

I knew she intended for me to use clearing the long-neglected path around the island—and *War and Peace* from Dad, I was presented with a large cardboard carton bearing oil stains around the bottom and those magic letters in bold blue on the sides: *Evinrude.* I tore it open to find a brand new 3.3-horsepower Sportwin outboard. Upon receipt of my all too lavish thanks, Mom winced, nodded toward Dad and said, "It was his idea."

Needless to say, I pressed the engine into service immediately. Much as I appreciated the Evinrude, however, I found myself longing for even more speed after a week of putt-putting around. I was being passed by everyone but Mom in the canoe. I simply had to have more power.

Fortuitously, my folks came to the same conclusion the following summer. Mom told us one night at supper how at Camp Wohelo she used to ride this plank that one of the counselors towed behind the camp launch. "It was just a couple boards cleated together, with a rope for a bridle," she said. "It's called an aquaplane." That was all I needed to hear.

"Could we make one?" I asked, my voice breaking into a falsetto.

"No, but *you* could," Mom replied. She sketched the device on a napkin, added dimensions, and shoved the paper in my direction. (Ordinarily, at this point I'd begin whining for assistance. But having recently completed a wretched wren house and several crooked pine daggers, I felt confident enough to tackle the project alone.) By late the next morning, I had the thing assembled, built from a rough pine plank and some spruce staging I found under the porch, a handful of galvanized screws, and a hank of hemp.

Mom had assured me that you didn't need a fast boat to tow an aquaplane, especially for someone as light as me—eighty pounds in waterlogged swim trunks.

With hopes high, I loaded my new creation into the Rangeley, grabbed a coil of rope for the tow line, and Mom and I headed out to the beach to test my handiwork. I set the aquaplane on the sand at the water's edge, and she idled south until the line became taut. By this time I was standing on the board, gripping the hemp with knuckles white. I nodded, Mom gunned the motor, and I slithered off the beach. The board and I zigged and zagged a few times before I splashed to starboard. After three tries with no success it became obvious that the little engine just couldn't cut it, and Mom made the pronouncement I'd been longing to hear: "We need more power." That evening it was decided: we would trade in our 3.3-horsepower Sportwin for a new 7 1/2-horsepower Fleetwin at Hartley's, where Dad had purchased the little Evinrude.

Scarcely moments after we brought the sleek engine home, I had it attached to the Rangeley's stern and shoved off. I immediately found the bow pointing at the sun (oh, the power of the Fleetwin).

After weighting the bow with fieldstones, the boat planed almost level with Mom at the helm in the stern, and I was up on the aquaplane on my first tug from the beach. With practice, I was able to start the board in deep water and was soon experimenting with tricks for my mother's benefit. She was less than amused, however, and would frown and shout from the helm, but I couldn't hear what she was saying over the roar of the engine. I'll never forget Mom's expression after a particularly foolhardy stunt as she pulled me from the water. She didn't say anything, but her face depicted this unforgettable mixture of anxiety and anger.

I laid low for a while to allow Mom to cool off, but we were soon back at it. I played it straight as long as I could, but couldn't resist my hotdog impulses. One brilliant late-summer afternoon while we were tooling around the lake, I let go of the bridle, went rigid, and slowly fell backwards into the wake. Mom surprised me by beaming. It was the first time I could remember getting past her rigid exterior. I'd made her smile. I had arrived.

Every time I hear that song, "I Wish't I Was in Peoria," home of Caterpillar Tractor Co., I'm reminded of an early March morning when old Caterpillar diesels set to work across the street. They were putting in a new subdivision, and the site crawled with activity. The chill of an overnight frost hung in the air, and the freshly disturbed earth smelled rich and musty. Twelve and trying to look inconspicuous, I stood behind a giant oak and watched the men get their dozers started.

It was a long ritual in the forties. Grease cups had to be filled then turned by hand to force the stringy stuff into the track idler wheel bearings, blade pivots and lifting gear. A good deal of hand oiling followed: track plates, exposed chains and gears, fan-drive pivots and much more got anointed with SAE 30. The men had to hand crank furnace oil from fifty-five gallon drums with rack-and-pinion pumps to fill the fuel tanks; the fuel dribbled from the hose nozzles as the men dragged them around, blending it with the moist soil, adding a sulfurous spice to the earth's aroma.

Caterpillar diesels were cranked with a pony engine, a small gasoline twin that started easily in cold weather. It nestled alongside the mother diesel and shared her cooling system to chase the chill from her bones. Its exhaust was routed through the diesel's intake manifold to preheat its first breaths. In return for the pony's warmth, mother diesel sheltered its vulnerable ignition from the elements and carried it about without complaint. Engine symbiosis.

On early Caterpillar diesels, the little ponies had to be hand-cranked; later models had electric starters. Several smart tugs usually did the trick. Choke closed, the pony's carburetor would drool on the first pull, accompanied by slurping noises. Choke opened a little, it would hit on the second or third try, sending staccato cracks of rifle fire into the crisp morning air. After a brief warm-up, the clutch was engaged, coupling the pony to the diesel.

Feeling the strain of the diesel's congealed oil, the pony's governor slammed its throttle wide open. With its compression weakened, the diesel began to turn over as the pony clattered in harness.

Once the diesel turned freely and developed oil pressure, it was time for old lazy bones to wake up. With the diesel's fuel rack opened wide and its compression reinstated, the poor pony nearly died from the strain but managed to keep it turning. Dense white smoke rings puffed from the diesel's tall, straight stack as the pony blasted on with all his might. Occasionally, a black puff joined the white, and the pony spun easier for a few turns. Gradually, black smoke replaced the white as mother diesel began to rumble deep inside. As the diesel came to life, the pony crackled faster and faster. Spewing a plume of grey and growling ferociously, the diesel's voice rose until checked by its governor then dropped to a hoarse, rolling gargle. With the pony's ignition cut, it panted to a halt, leaving mother diesel to do all the talking. And what a thrilling song it was, ringing unfettered from its straight-through exhaust, rising and falling in response to the fluctuating load.

The men enjoyed it, too. They drove machines with soul, whose long-stroke engines lugged incredibly, moving deep-rooted boulders with satisfying surges as the earth rolled up in front of their blades. Tree stumps popped from the soil as easily as bubbles leave champagne. I cheered quietly from the sidelines as each obstacle was conquered.

* * * * * *

Much as I love the old Caterpillar diesel dozers, it's the Caterpillar road graders that captivate me. Tall and spindly, these iron mantises arch their trussed frames over the road ahead, banking their front wheels steeply as they follow the turns. Above the driver's lofty, exposed perch two thirds of the way back, a quaint, curved, sheet iron canopy spreads its shade. The tall diesel engine brings up the rear, terminated by the famous Caterpillar radiator. Under the engine, I could see the exposed yellow flywheel, besmirched with grease, steadily churning.

Following an aged Caterpillar diesel grader cruising between jobs in transit gear was a feast in sight and sound. The engine's sensitive governor reacted to every bump, every change of grade, however slight. Modulating its melancholy, two note song, it positioned its weighted exhaust rain cap first wide open then at forty-five degrees as the giant insect dithered and wobbled ahead, tossing its driver again and again into the rafters. How I longed to trade places with its pilot.

* * * * * *

Late one afternoon, I almost got my chance. After the workmen had gone home, my buddy Garrison Stover and I returned to haunt the subdivision site. Gary, stocky and muscular, with an almost beautiful face topped with cropped, sandy hair, stood in sharp contrast to me, a lean, gawky rodent, complete with exposed incisors and runaway acne.

Gary had studied Caterpillar operating procedures too, and thought he knew enough to start one up. After checking to make sure that we were alone, he approached one of the newer dozers with an electric starting pony engine. Twiddling the choke and ignition switch while cranking, he managed to get a few pops and one desultory report before hopelessly flooding the thing. I ran like hell, figuring the blast would surely arouse one of the neighbors. Gary scurried off in another direction. We compared notes later over a cup of cocoa in the kitchen.

Gary said he'd seen the workmen switch the ignition on and off during a starting attempt. I claimed with equal confidence that his procedure made no sense. Although I had not witnessed a start on Gary's chosen dozer, I felt sure of one thing: the pony engine needed much less choking. On that we agreed. Tomorrow we'd try again.

We never got a second chance. Gary had inadvertently left the ignition switch on. The next afternoon we were greeted with a sorry sight. Our target stood cold and partly disassembled in the same spot we had left it; the other machines were still warm and smelling of fresh number 2D. The men had taken off the pony's distributor cap, and the points were missing. The battery had disappeared as well.

The color faded from Gary's face. I felt a knot tighten in my stomach. As we shuffled back home, kicking the dirt ahead of us, heads bowed in thought, I took a solemn oath never to hurt another engine as long as I lived.

Charley Watkins

South Casco, Maine, July 1954. When I was seventeen and working at Gulick's camp Little Wohelo on Raymond Cape, I spent my free time scouting the countryside for one-lungers. Ossie Jewett, the camp's caretaker, got wind of my obsession with antique one-cylinder engines and gave me a tip. Back in the thirties, he remembered, Charley Watkins cut ice from Sebago Lake with a buzz saw powered by one. "I'll bet he's still got that engine," Ossie mused.

I wasted no time pursuing Ossie's lead. Arriving at dusk at WATKINS HOUSE AND CABINS, a rambling white farmhouse on Cape Road, I found a scrap of paper tacked to the kitchen doorjamb below a rotary switch. The note, scribbled in a shaky hand, read: "I am asleep upstairs. If you need me, throw this switch. It will start a fan by my bed and wake me. I'll be down in a few minutes."

It seemed cruel to wake him. Besides, Ossie had warned me Charley could be ornery. He lived alone, never married. Years ago, after falling asleep at the wheel and driving his Model A coupe into a ditch, he stored the flivver in his father's carriage house and never drove again. Now in his mid-sixties, he walked every day to Maines's Store in South Casco for his mail and groceries.

Deciding to risk rejection for the sake of an engine, I snapped the switch and waited. Sounds of scuffling erupted over the pantry, followed by labored clumping on the stairs. The door opened, revealing the drawn moon face of a man whose china blue eyes searched mine. "Yes?" he screeched.

Noticing the bulky hearing aid on his huge left ear inclined toward me, I shouted, "Sorry to wake you, sir. I'm Kevin Sheehan, work over at Gulick's. I understand you used to have a one-cylinder engine for cutting ice."

"Yuh. I worked many years for Dr. and Mrs. Gulick, cutting ice and filling the ice houses at their camps. They liked and trusted me."

"Well, sir, I don't suppose you have much use for that engine anymore?"

"Yuh."

"Would you consider parting with it, perhaps?"

Charley didn't answer right away. He kicked at the finial door stopper then eyeballed me closely, sizing up my integrity.

He'd think about it, he said. I should come back on Saturday. He'd have his answer then. I thanked him and left.

Saturday being my day off and figuring Charley for an early riser, I arrived at seven. This time I found an envelope tacked to the doorjamb, addressed in the same scrawl.

This letter is for the boy who is going to have the engine. So when you come you read it.

Inside the envelope I found this note:

Clarence has been here with his truck, and he says his truck body is too high, and he don't want to haul it. Now this is all I can do. You will have to get the engine down yourself somehow. Why don't you try and get Gulick's truck. Awful reasonable where you work. Now I have left the house door unlocked here so you can go in and look the engine over all you please. When you leave here you close the doors. When you get a truck I will help you load it on the best I can. You can come here any time you please and work on the engine. Charley.

When you are in the house just don't smoke for I am afraid of fire, but I don't think you smoke anyway. You are a good boy and I like to have you around here.

Uncomfortable entering the house in his absence, I drove to the store for an Orange Crush. There he was, plodding all stooped over with a sack on his back. I offered him a ride but he waved me off, so I went for the soda to allow him time to arrive home in dignity.

When I got back, Charley was doing his wash in the kitchen. He came to the door grinning like a sickle moon. "I'll just be a minute here," he squawked. I gladly waited.

As we walked back through the house to the attached barn, Charley put his arm around my shoulder and tugged me toward him. "You're an awful nice boy. I want you to have the engine." His voice was querulous, he sprayed me with saliva, and his breath smelled of onions, but I didn't mind.

There, in a cobwebbed corner under a pile of burlap sacks rested the engine, a six-horse Fairbanks-Morse. Charley wiped the dust from the oval tag on its hopper displaying a large letter Z. "She's good," he shouted. "Ain't froze up."

I tugged at one of the twin flywheels. It rolled easily, welling a sigh from the exhaust elbow. "I'll take her," I said, struggling to choke back tears.

I gave Charley his asking price: fifteen dollars, a paltry sum for my priceless iron friend. We agreed that Ossie and I would return in the afternoon to haul it away with the camp GMC. When we came back for the engine, Charley made me promise to return and stay in his best cabin for the night. No charge.

I procrastinated until nearly nine before leaving camp, half hoping Charley'd forgotten the invitation, but he had left another envelope at the door addressed to "The Engine Boy." Inside, he'd tucked the key to his largest cabin, an octagonal shanty perched on a granite outcrop just behind the house. It was the only cabin lighted.

A round braided rug dominated the spotless single room. An oil heater opposite the bed poked its chimney out a window. The tiny icebox stood empty except for a note from Charley. *"Breakfast at seven. Please come."* How could I refuse?

Sunday morning I found Charley in the kitchen, cooking. The table was set for two. "Eat up all good," he shrieked, handing me a plateful of eggs, bacon and blueberry muffins. "Don't get to cook for guests much anymore. Most folks, they're not so nice to me as you. You stay here anytime. You're an awful nice boy." My breakfast got all blurry. I'd never had anyone say that before, even once.

* * * * * *

I couldn't bring myself to stop at Charley's again for fear I'd break down and make a fool of myself. But every now and then I'd pass him trudging Raymond Cape Road. He'd wave with a desperately animated gesture as if I were the only friend he had in the world. Perhaps I was.

Danceing (sic)

Varney, Maine, November 24, 1956. By suppertime the night sky has peeled the blankets from the land. Wood smoke veils the farms, most of the church, Warren's store, and Libby's Garage. Only the baleful howl of Jake Mellen's coonhound pursuing a rabbit behind the parsonage disturbs the windless night.

The grange stands in the clear atop a rise on Route 22. If you face the weathered sign staked on the front lawn, the one lettered by the cub scouts—*Danceing, Saturday, 8:30 to 12*—Orion hovers in sharp relief just over the chimney.

It's 6:30 on the Saturday after Thanksgiving, and Dot Quimby has already arrived to fire the grange stoves and set up the kitchen. Lights are glowing behind the manila blinds in the mess hall.

At eight o'clock, Loring Murch noses his AA 1929 Ford into the desiccated milkweed stalks under the second story bump-out washroom. Witte and I, riding in the truck bed, instinctively duck the soil pipes overhead. (The grange raised just enough money by raffling off quilts and Christmas ornaments made by the ladies to add plumbing in September.) Dot's 1950 Chevy, the only other car in the field, is already etched in frost.

Loring depresses the ignition plunger, and the engine chuffs to a sigh. He bends to close the fuel tap under the tank before dismounting, circles the truck and opens the passenger door for his wife.

"You look pretty slick in that outfit, Ida. Smell good, too."

Ida emits a juicy hiss as she alights and waves him off with her left hand while juggling an apple pie with her right. "Aw go on with yuh."

Witte and I jump off the tailgate and follow Ida to the grange. Loring stumps along behind us, keeping a watchful eye on his amorous daughter. As we enter, Dot hails us from the kitchen. "How you folks, tonight?"

"Goood," Loring bellows from the coat room.

Ida shuffles to the pantry, lays her still-warm pie on the counter and busies herself setting the tables. Witte makes a bee line for the potbelly and rubs her hands above the lid. I go upstairs to look around.

The rock maple dance floor is framed by white wainscoted walls. Milky pendant fixtures cast the room in a pasty pallor. At the far end is a stage with an upright Sterling piano dressed in a serpentine case, its exposed ivories cracked and yellow with age. The two millers Loring swatted in mid-September still lie on its lid. Benches under the stern portraits of Washington, Lincoln and several salient past masters of the grange run along each sidewall. The embossed tin ceiling, figured in decorative squares, has received too many coats of cream enamel. Each collar tie is festooned with colored lights. And on the back wall, near the stairs, an Alna Number Two log stove chortles on its diet of oak. I stand near it for a moment and warm to this scene, preserved from an era that passed my hometown in Connecticut thirty years ago.

Alice and Royal Lombard arrive at 8:15 and situate themselves on the landing, halfway up the stairs. He sits at a card table, taking the dollar admission and greeting each couple by their first names as they ascend. Alice stands alongside, passing out the tickets, advising everyone to save their stubs for the drawing at eleven o'clock. It's hard to get around them, especially for the ladies in crinolines. I suspect they planned it that way.

I head downstairs after the Lombard encampment sets up and have a lot of explaining to do. Fortunately, Witte is on her way up to get me. I had just finished telling Royal about my friendship with the piano player's daughter when Witte reaches the landing. "Karcher and I are goin' steady. He's stayin' with us for the holidays." I blush hearing Witte confirm our relationship in public.

As we turn to climb the last steps, the Murch ensemble opens with the love waltz, "Diane," from the film, *Seventh Heaven*. The house lights dim. It's precisely eight thirty. The few couples that got by us during my induction are already scuffing about the floor as we enter the ballroom.

Danceing (sic)

For a second, I think I'm back in fifth grade, attending a Christmas concert in the auditorium. There is the band on its orange lit stage playing not quite in tune. There are the strings of colored lights. There are the patriotic portraits hiding in the shadows. There are the ceiling fans barely turning.

And there is Loring, bent over the keyboard, squinting in the dim light, his aquiline nose almost touching the music rack before him. As his slender fingers work the keys, he chews his cud so that his prominent chin keeps time with the music. Although he resembles a hawk in profile, talons deployed, pouncing on his prey, the brittle, ornate embellishments ringing from the old Sterling are those from the throat of a thrush. Transfixed by the dichotomy, I can't take my eyes off of him.

We are sitting on the south bench under the stern portrait of Herman Strout, who, according to the inscription, presided from 1918 to 1923. I hear a breathy voice in my right ear, "Dance with me, deah."

"Uh…sorry, I was watching your dad. He really has the touch."

When I don't move to stand, Witte slides away along the bench to give herself room to focus. Her sable hair is draped over one eye like Veronica Lake. "Well?"

Notwithstanding Mrs. Graham Todd Johnston's dancing lessons to which my parents subjected me at age thirteen, I avoid fast numbers, but here I have no excuse; the band plays only fox-trots, waltzes, and the occasional polka.

Loring begins *Night and Day*, omitting the monotonous verse which he apparently dislikes. I rise and offer my hand to Witte. She stands but does not approach. I watch her upper lip curl and her chest rise with anticipation as I advance and take her in my arms in closed ballroom position.

Visions of Peggy Lovendale, my voluptuous class partner, and Mrs. Johnston, my cockatoo instructress with recumbent crest, flood back as I touch Witte's taffeta. I begin counting quietly, *One, two… One, two… Side close*, strutting mechanically about, back rigid, scanning the floor for obstacles.

Witte tolerates my robotic behavior for several measures then stops, backs away and places both hands on her hips. "Now look, I wanna man, not a machine."

"Hey, I know I'm no Fred Astaire, but I do have feelings. Keep it up and you'll be looking for another partner."

Witte drops her hands and gasps. I become aware that the other dancers are staring at us. My date looks at the floor and pouts. "I don't want another pahtner."

What she gets is a whole bunch of partners. The house lights snap on and reed man Wendell Guptill blows a cadenza on his soprano sax en chemade. Loring wheels around on his piano stool and hollers, "Get your partners for the *Lady of the Lake*."

Couples begin forming two lines perpendicular to the stage, guys on the right, gals on the left. I try to escape, but Witte drags me into the fray, pulling off her red pumps and scaling them under the bench on the way.

At Loring's command, every other person crosses over. Witte counts heads and advances confidently as she grinds toward me. I step off to meet her half way. As we pass, she bumps me with her hip and recedes chuckling. From across the room, I watch her greet several of the regulars in the other line; she seems to know them all.

A small, immaculate man in his sixties is dressed in a double-breasted suit so crisp that it looks like it just came from the cleaners. He moves stiffly as if he suffers from a prostate infection. Witte tells me that Moe used to sing at a nightclub in Portland. Now he occasionally adds his tremulous tenor to the Murch ensemble. His repertoire consists mainly of gaslight songs, but he confines himself to the old standards on Saturday nights in Varney.

Moe corners Witte and me in the vestibule late in the evening. He hasn't been asked to sing and looks crestfallen. Vise-gripping Witte's shoulder with a shaky hand, he moves close to her ear and croaks, "My wife left me for my father. Guess I wasn't old enough for her."

Witte winces, pries herself free of Moe and rolls her eyes at me. "He's drunk, Karcher. Let's go." She tows me back onto the floor and clamps me in her arms for her dad's rousing version of the *Johnson Rag*.

While we bounce along to the repetitious fox-trot, Witte tells me that Kendall Maines, just ahead of us, is a grave digger. During the waltzes and fox-trots, he and his wife Nora follow an imaginary track around the perimeter of the hall, chugging counterclockwise down each side and pirouetting precisely twice at each corner like dolls on a music box stage. In brush cut and sports jacket, Ken leads with his forehead pressed firmly against hers, head bowed, jaw set, left arm bent at a perfect right angle as if he was signaling.

I learn that Willard is a displaced cowboy. Smelling strongly of himself and the farm he works, he arrives at the dance just as he leaves the barn, dressed in riding boots, pegged jeans, denim western shirt and a bandana around his neck. From his belt hangs a raft of tools: a hunting knife, pipe scraper and tamper, numerous keys, and a duck call. His red tobacco pouch sticks out a back pocket like a sore thumb. Will stoops as if embarrassed by his height, which Witte says is only a little over six feet. A great deal of his time is spent in the vestibule doorway, making love to a corncob pipe. For all that, the women compete to lure him to dance. Several times, I hear him shout to one of the advancing ladies, "I'm…not…goin'…to do it."

There is another man whom at first I confuse with Will. He has the same wiry build and posture but different habits. Ronald wears a weak, twisted smile and seems unsure of himself. His most salient feature is a shock of jet black hair that projects forward, shading his forehead like a visor. He is wearing a soft cotton chamois shirt and penny loafers. Ron is single. His following is limited to the twin sisters from Gorham, Beth and Janet Angola, both older than himself.

Beth is the feisty one with long, straight, golden brown hair. She has a dynamite figure from the waist up but too much bottom. That doesn't stop her from cutting up the floor with forceful dips and dives. Unless you are pretty strong, Beth does the leading. I'm sure she back-leads Ronald.

Janet wears spectacles, dresses older than her age and moves with reserve on the floor. There is never any lost motion in her step, yet she does not inhibit her partner. Ronald seems to find her subtlety arousing, judging by his expression when they dance. Ronald is with Janet for the jig.

Witte winks at me from across the room as Loring orders the first call: "Balance the next be-low." I grab the mousy little old woman on my left and begin to swing her. Much to my surprise, she spins like a top, pushing off vigorously with her tiny, muscular feet. I'll never judge a Maine woman by her appearance after that.

The reel goes better than I expected, and Witte seems pleased with my performance. Her encouraging smiles, flashed from various parts of the hall as she whirls in the arms of her compatriots, help me relax.

At about the halfway point, I become distracted by the comical antics of a ruddy-faced farmer who makes a show of conserving energy. Each time he becomes sidelined in the reel, he sidles over to the nearest bench and sits down. When the dance calls for his presence again, he jumps up and takes his place, pretending that he was there all the time.

The contra abruptly ends, the lights dim, and we all fall to the benches. Puffing and exhilarated, Witte blurts between gasps, "You were wonderful, deah." Her hair is streaked with perspiration, and a few strands stick to her moist cheeks. "I gotta cool off. You, too." Before I can object, Witte tows me off the bench and heads us for the stairs. At the front door, she swings a shawl around her shoulders and steps out into the frosty night. I lurch after her, turn up my collar and plunge my hands deep into my pockets. We circle the grange slowly, crunching the rye stubble, listening to strains of the waltz, *God's Little Candles*, leak out of the drafty building.

Half way around, I stop. Framed in the solitary backstage window high above us is Loring, hunched over the keys, chomping as he plays, a portrait that will hang in my mind's gallery forever.

Once around the grange is enough. Without coats, the twenty-degree clear night cools us down fast, and Witte's heels are no match for the tufted field. "Maine women only wear pumps on special occasions. I should know better."

We enter the mess hall through the side door to slurp some water from the fountain. The place is deserted except for Dot and her husband Dan playing rummy in the kitchen. The waltz set has ended. Witte slides into a folding chair at one of the long tables, puffs her cheeks and forces a full breath past her pursed lips. "Woof, it's nippy out there."

Upstairs, I hear Loring strike the opening chords of Carmen Lombardo's *Boo Hoo (You've got me crying for you)*. There is a brief scuffling overhead. Then the old sugar maple ceiling bursts into resonance, driven by a hundred and twenty feet trudging in unison. Like the soundboard of a Steinway D, its broad, well-seasoned expanse amplifies every beat of the fox-trot. I duck reflexively. Witte chuckles. "Floor's been up there forty years, Karcher. Guess it'll last the night." She stands. "It's nearly intermission; let's catch the Circle Waltz." I follow her to the stairs, far enough behind to enjoy the lunge and sway of her well-oiled motion.

"It's a mixer, like Musical Chairs," Witte calls over her shoulder as we crest the stairs. In the vestibule, she pauses to explain. "When the music stops, everyone forms a circle and begins a grand right and left, girls moving clockwise, men counterclockwise, pulling by, hand over hand, until the music stops again. Then you're supposed to dance with the new person in front of you." She smirks. "'Course there's lots of cheatin'. You gotta be quick to get a good-un."

"You know I don't like competition, Witte. Especially when it's random."

"Oh, come on, now. It's fun." Hearing her dad call the set, she tugs me onto the floor, spins to face me and waits for me to take her in my arms.

"Not this time. You're on your own." I bench myself to avoid certain embarrassment.

"Suit yourself."

Witte snaps an about face and aims for Norman, who is shuffling uneasily alone in the northeast corner. From where I sit, it looks as if Norman and Witte have known each other for a long time and fairly intimately. Their animated conversation, gestures and smiles are hard enough to swallow, but when I see them embrace and commence to dance, I can stand it no longer. As the rage hits me, I bolt from the ballroom, take the stairs two at a time and set off down the street at a four-minute-mile pace.

When I reach Warren's, I slow to a jog, remembering that one-cylinder engines are dependable, never fickle like a woman. Given loving attention, one-lungers behave predictably and remain loyal. The thought slows me to a brisk walk.

Come to think of it, *I* have that kind of fidelity and consistency. Like an engine, my body chugs along steadily and reliably. My behavior is unambiguous and consistent. I never lie or deceive. You know what you're getting when you choose me.

I'm swaggering as I turn back toward the grange. "I'll show her who's boss. No one's going to kick the Engine Boy around anymore."

Despite the bracing night, by the time I reach the lobby I'm warm as toast. It's intermission, and everyone is downstairs munching Jordan's hot dogs and pie and slurping coffee. Witte is already stuffing herself alongside Norman. Loring is standing at her back, patting her shoulder while he chats with Myra on her left. As I sneak behind them, I hear Myra complain about the loud saxophone player, and Loring explain that Wendell played in the Marine Band. "That's why he blows so hard."

Ida, who is serving behind the counter, sees me coming for the last wedge of banana cream. Shielding it from several groping hands, she greets me warmly. "Karcher, deah. I saved this one 'specially, remembering how you like it." She smiles hopefully. "Havin' a good time?"

"Oh, yes. Thanks. I love this place, especially Loring's music." Witte isn't even on my list of likes, let alone at the top.

I find a seat at the table on the other side of the room from Witte and face her, occasionally glancing up from my pie without lifting my head, so she won't notice.

Loring has moved on to stand behind Melody Church at the next table. He's listening with restrained glee to Orrin, her husband, tell about the troubles he's having with his GMC. Loring is strictly a Ford man.

Witte is engrossed in conversation with Norman who seems to be punctuating his narrative with obscene gestures. I hope he's just relating how he was cut off at an intersection but fear it is a lurid tale of passion—unrequited, I promise myself—that he holds for her.

Oops, she's caught me looking at her. I see her wink a split second before I divert my eyes. She has finished eating and is leaning over to make a closing statement to Norman before standing. I make sure not to look again, in an attempt to keep her on ice a little longer.

As I raise my fork to shove the last piece of banana filling into my mouth, I feel a warm, taut belly press against my back, then little palms sliding down my chest. I put the fork down, lean back and lay my head in a fragrant and sumptuous cradle. When I look up, I see the angelic face of an upside down doll with huge, serious eyes staring down at me.

"You mad at me?" says the doll in dulcet tones with tortured expression. I stretch a hand and stroke its cheek. It smiles upside down at me. When I nuzzle my head in its cleavage, it sighs and squirms and tickles my neck with its fingernails, sending shivers up my spine. I reach for its hands and cup them to my lips. When I kiss them, it shivers just like me.

I gulp the last swig of my coffee and rise to face my tormentor. I would have to have been robbed of all senses to miss Witte's body language. With difficulty she forms the words she whispers in my ear. "There's a little room off the stage where they keep the band instruments. I got a key. No one goes in there till after midnight when they lock up the horns, drums and guitar."

I feel the blood rush to my groin as I listen to the details of her plot. We are to tell her folks that we're going for a walk, that we will be back at midnight in time to help clean up, that we need a chance to talk on our last night together. Then, before the band reconvenes, we are to slip backstage, lock ourselves into the closet and do it.

With intermission almost over, Witte corners her folks one at a time and sets them up while I hit the head. We go through the motions of putting on our coats and leaving by the front door. Then we creep around the building in the shadow of the eaves and reenter by the fire escape that runs up the north side to the stage hall. After verifying that no one is about, we sneak backstage and unlock the closet.

There is no light inside except that which finds its way under the door, so we have to move about carefully until our eyes adjust to the dark—just long enough for a standing hug and grope.

Hearing voices approaching, we smother our moans and giggles. Loring is discussing the repertoire for the remainder of the evening with Wendell. Witte stifles a snicker, hearing Wendell mention that Myra has again requested "There's a Trick in Pickin' a Chick, Chick Chicken."

Witte sets about spreading our coats on the floor like a geisha preparing the bed for her master. She plumps the collar of her coat and overlays it with her angora shawl, then smooths every wrinkle from my jacket and positions the sleeves so as to leave no lumps. It takes several minutes to adjust everything to her liking.

I'm taking this all in while sitting on one of the drum cases. As she swoops about, bending here, crouching there, every motion flows from the last as if it belongs to the same ballet. There's never an unfair curve in her extremities. She appears to be perpetually dancing.

Nesting complete, Witte sits demurely on our coats and pats the spot she has selected for me with her outstretched palm, fingers reflexed to protect her long, oval nails unspoiled by polish. I bend down, catch her hand and begin devouring her fingers, one at a time. When she exhales a protracted sigh, I start to feel dizzy and decide to sit down before I fall and reveal our hideaway.

I'm not feeling well. I'm trembling and my hands are freezing. I heave several deep breaths to quell a wave of nausea and hope that Witte doesn't detect my discomfort.

Danceing (sic)

It terrifies me to lose control so easily. I pride myself in always remaining grounded and predictable as an engine. If I let my feelings take over, there is the very real danger of my being overcome by disease and possibly death. I have to be vigilant to be sure no one, no thing gets the better of me. If I let my guard down, even for a second, disaster, waiting in the wings, can work its worst.

What a time to have a case of nerves.

Witte draws me to her, nuzzles me about the neck and whispers, "You don't have to do anything you don't feel like, deah."

I feel so ashamed, wasting my last precious opportunity to make love to her. It makes me furious. Turning on her, I stammer through clenched teeth, "You.... You planned this, didn't you? ...to make me break down. How dare you? You have no right to manipulate me. I'm not your puppet...Pull my strings and I'll perform for you. Hah! Who do you think I am, anyway? Some kind of a gigolo?"

Witte just holds me tighter. In a voice as calm as Sebago Lake on a windless night, she soothes, "Believe it or not, love will still your fears and melt your anger." She pauses. "I'm not talkin' 'bout sex, Karcher; I'm talkin' 'bout lovin' yourself. Your trouble, deah, is that you don't think much of Karcher."

That certainly isn't the response I expected. It's the truth. The accuracy of her observation is inescapable, and my reaction surprises us both.

A brutal wave of passion hits me, and I shove Witte down on the floor. Fortunately, her head hits the padded shawl, spilling her hair over the soft, white wool like ink from an upset vial. She stares up at me, gasping, face flushed, eyes wide with terror.

With a powerful backhand to her right shoulder, I flip her over and buzz her zipper to its stop. Her back arches involuntarily. When I see her shoulders sink to the floor, I know she has given up.

Clamping my hands wide on her hips, I spin her over again, like I do to start a one-lunger. She cries softly for help as her head comes to rest facing me.

Danceing (sic)

* * * * * *

The music stops as I finish pulling on my last shoe. Witte, the speedy dresser, is trying to comb her tangled locks into some semblance of order with a plastic comb that resembles a rake. We hear the bump of instruments being shut in their cases. There isn't a moment to lose.

I ease open the door a crack and peek out. It's then that I notice the air in the dance hall smells quite different than the atmosphere in the closet. In the heat of passion, Witte and I have generated a suggestive musk that escapes our fatigued olfactory senses until contrasted with the locker room odor of simple exertion exuded by the dancers. I want to fan the door to mix the two flavors, but there isn't time.

Seeing no one in the hall, I beckon Witte to follow me. Stealthily, we slip out, making sure to lock the door. We head straight for the fire escape and blend with the throng of tired dancers slowly wending their way down the wrought iron stairway. I'm certain we have been undiscovered until Loring meets us at the truck.

Confronting us with head lowered, he looks over his imaginary half-frames. "Band closet's awful small for dancin'."

Diaphone

Kettle Cove, Cape Elizabeth, Maine. August 9, 1953. Tall, amply developed, shirtwaisted and poured into a pair of 505 Levis, she picks her way among the beach pebbles, now and then bending to select a feldspar treasure. The onshore breeze sets her long, dark hair roiling, which she repeatedly sweeps away to clear her vision. Behind her and not far out to sea, a fog bank looms.

Sixteen and salacious with a fresh driver's license and far from flush, having purchased a 1930 Tudor Ford with a cracked block for seventy-five dollars from a seedy garage at Pride's Corner, I hit the road. The flivver gets me to Cape Elizabeth before boiling over and hammering fearfully. After a stop to refill the radiator, I succeed in coaxing it to the shore.

"Hi," I call, stepping out of my steaming jalopy.

The girl makes no acknowledgement.

Boldly bursting from the dune grasses, I stride toward her. "Would you like a lift?"

The girl stops and scowls. "Do I know you?"

Oh, boy. This isn't the first time I heard those words from a girl my age. When I was ten, a girl helping her uncles to run a sawmill in Wilton, Connecticut, asked me that same question when I expressed admiration for her prowess in tending the engine. Now, six years older and brimming with testosterone, I'm determined not to let another female sass me.

"That fog bank looks to be coming ashore. I didn't see your car and figured you might need a ride."

"You askin' me to ride in *that?*" The girl points accusingly at the Ford.

"Let me try again. I'm Karcher Stickney from Connecticut. I'm working at a girl's camp on Raymond Cape for the summer. When I saw you, alone and with no visible means of transportation, I…"

"Now look, I live on the Two Lights road. I'm on foot and I like it that way."

"Sorry, I didn't get your name."

"Whadda *you* care? You'll never see me again."

"On the contrary, I'd like to get to know you better."

Judging from her indelible frown, the girl looks to be a year or two older than I am—a pugnacious beauty, irresistibly challenging.

Without hesitation, she snaps an about face, tosses her hair, and marches away. "Fat chance, fella," she calls over her shoulder.

My groin tempts me to chase her, but my brain urges caution. This girl looks too good to lose by my being aggressive. If I pursue a female this feisty, she might never give me a second chance. But as I stand there, watching her recede to a speck, my libido takes command.

Let me see; she said she lives on the Two Lights road. Maybe I can overtake her before she disappears into her house. The Ford has cooled sufficiently for me to top up the radiator but not enough to free the pistons from their bores. When I tromp the starter, it just clunks. Nothing to do but wait.

A good half hour passes before the engine will turn over, and then it starts reluctantly one cylinder at a time while spewing a cloud of blue smoke from the tailpipe. Sensing its end is near, I launch it gently using just a whiff of throttle. If I'm careful, it might get me back to camp. Since it's now almost nine o'clock with a fog bank approaching, I know I ought to get going. The Ford's dim headlights are barely adequate on a clear night.

Concerned, I start heading home, but lust again overwhelms my better judgment, and I turn right at the sign pointing to Two Lights State Park. I have to find that girl.

It's almost dark. A few stars are poking through the mist. Lights are already glowing in the houses on Two Lights Road, but I have no idea which one belongs to the girl. Certainly she must be home by now. But even if I'd seen her enter her house, I wouldn't dare knock and ask for her. I don't even know her name.

Several cars pass me as I chuff along the shoulder, craning my neck to catch a glimpse of her in one of the lighted windows. Minutes later, I find myself at a dead end. In my futile search, I traverse more than a mile of the narrow, winding tar road that passes the state park and leads downhill to a cul-de-sac seaward of the two lighthouses.

Discouraged, I park at the foot of a square brick building on a point of land east of the two towers, and get out. The sea surrounds me; its swells crash and hiss as they strike the shale ledges below. A flock of gulls are perched on a large outcrop, all facing into the wind. In the twilight, the silently advancing fog bank looks ominous as a thunderhead. I draw a deep breath of salt air and sigh. "Faint heart never won fair lady," I mutter.

"Can't you read?" comes a contralto close behind me.

I jump and spin around. The girl I'd been looking for is standing on a rock not two yards away, pointing at a sign near the blockhouse:

KEEP AWAY: HEARING DAMAGE
SIGNAL SOUNDS WITHOUT WARNING

"Oh, it's you," I say, feeling awkward. "I assumed you'd be snug inside on a night like this. What are you doing out here, anyway?"

"Same question to you, buddy."

"I was enjoying the sea before you startled me."

"Stahtled? You have no idea. When that fog gets here, you'll be more'n stahtled."

"Have you lived here long, this close to the sea?"

"Yuh. Father's a lobsterman. He's out there now, pullin' the last of his traps. See that red light? That's him, headin' in. Hope the fog don't catch him."

"It's getting chilly. Why don't we sit in the car until your dad's safely in the channel?"

The girl hesitates, but as the first wisps of fog swirl over the blockhouse, her expression softens.

"I still don't know your name," I say, opening the passenger door for her.

"Just call me Cory." She slides into the right front seat and closes the door before I have a chance to. I circle the car and get behind the wheel.

Even with the Ford's windows open a couple inches, the engine's blowby still clouds the cab sufficiently to elicit a cough and a comment from my passenger. "Gawd! You tryin' to kill us?" She begins cranking her window down the rest of the way.

Despite the residual hydrocarbon haze, I can smell her feminine perspiration. Her breathing sounds labored, and I can feel her warm exhaust on my arm as I reach over to help her lower the window. When my elbow inadvertently grazes her breast, I'm afraid she'll leave, but she simply squirms in her seat.

I just finish straightening myself behind the wheel when I see the blockhouse lights snap on and then momentarily dim as a commotion commences inside the brick building. Fascinated, I bolt from the Ford, dash to the cobwebbed rear window and peer in. Cory is right behind me, tugging at my shirt and yelling. "You crazy? Come on; let's get the hell out of here before that thing goes off."

"But look; it's just a big air compressor, probably pumping up those tanks in the corner." I put my ear to the glass to better enjoy the one-cylinder compressor's measured thumping and honking.

"Hurry," Cory shouts in my other ear before making a dash for the Ford and frantically cranking up the window. And not a moment too soon.

A tremendous roar erupts from somewhere in front of the building. I jump back from the window, ducking instinctively, hands clamped over my ears. "Holy shit!"

A couple seconds later, the thing bellows again and, after another short pause, a third time. Each outcry slides a semitone lower in pitch than the one preceding. Then an eerie silence. Crouching low with my ears tightly plugged, I creep around to the front of the blockhouse. There, overhead, I see a pair of cast iron, double-mouthed trumpets pointing out to sea. Hearing the compressor continue chugging steadily inside, I recover my ears, scurry under the horns and stand with my back to the façade. My heart is pounding and I'm shaking uncontrollably.

I don't have to wait long before the behemoth assaults me again, and again, and again. After the second group of blasts passes, I realize that no physical attack has followed them. With that comforting thought, I become analytical. The outbursts seem to follow a pattern. I look at my watch and wait. When the sweep second hand passes the four, the monster speaks again. I flinch at the percussive impact but manage to follow the dial as I time the interval between each group of blasts. Exactly a minute elapses each time.

At close range, the creature doesn't simply roar; it spits and gargles, snaps and hisses. All the upper partials are present along with the fundamental. Its voice is raw, harsh and venomous. And the strangest part of all is the way each guttural outcry ends in a profound grunt like the lowest note of the contrabassoon.

By now the fog bank has blanketed the point, and the lights from the two towers are no longer visible. Timing my departure to follow the last and deepest grunt of the foghorn's trilogy, I grope my way around the building and down to the Ford. I get in and shut the door.

She's gone.

Visibility having shrunk to no more than a yard, I sit entombed in my dying flivver with just Cory's scent and the diaphone to keep me company.

Didn't Hurt

Orr's Island, Maine, winter 1947. Cora Lombard clutches a coffee mug as she rocks alongside her Atlantic wood range. Outside, a nor'easter howls, piling drifts against the attached woodshed. The late January storm has already dropped a foot of snow since daybreak, and the wind-whipped powder has almost obscured her view out the kitchen window of Gordon's lobster traps stacked on the dock, ready for next season's catch.

She greets me with a smile when I let myself in but quickly becomes all business, peering over her half-frames. "Shut that door quick, Kevun, before Ole Man Winter gets any closer. Gorry, we don't see you for a month, and you turn up on a mornin' like this. Don't tell me you're gettin' cabin fever; winter's not half over."

At sixty-six, there's a lot more life left in Cora than she wants me to see. A tattered navy shawl shrouds her firm curves, no rouge tinges her taut cheeks, and her fine, long hair, barely streaked with silver, is wound tight in a snood. She puts down her mug and stands without effort. "You look all froze up, deah. Sit down and have some coffee."

"I can't stay, Cora. Arvilla's run out the water, and the auxiliary well pump needs a new impeller. I'm on my way to Reynolds Hardware to get a replacement. Just stopped by to see if you need anything."

Without answering, Cora hands me a steaming mug of Savarin, pulls another chair up to the stove and returns to her rocker. Her deep-set dark brown eyes study me. After an awkward pause, she says, "We don't need anything in town, Kevun. Stay for some soup. Gordon's out in the barn, working on your skiff. Reckon he's 'bout nailed the bottom on by now. He should be in for lunch in fifteen, ten minutes."

"No, thanks, Cora. I've got a domestic emergency on my hands. You know how Arvilla frets when she loses the amenities. How far is it to Drab Mills?"

Cora squints at the snow swirling outside the window before answering. "Today? 'Bout two hours."

I take one last sip of my coffee and stand. "Thanks for the warmup, Cora. Tell Gordon I'll be over after the storm to help him turn the skiff over for its interior decorating." I start for the door.

"Land's sakes, Kevun. Can't you sit still for a minute? Tell me about your Christmas. Did you two lovebirds go skiing?"

I'm now on one leg. I tell her we did and as little else of our holiday as I think I can get away with, but there's no stopping her now.

"Our six-year-old grandson Buffy was here over Christmas," she says after I agree to a second cup of coffee. "He's spoilt, you know. Into everything. Gordon don't like him. Never has.

"Well, you know how boys are. Didn't take him long to find Gordon's Lionel trains in the attic. Gordon warned him, if he went up there he'd get a lickin'. Naturally, that little tyke ran right up the stairs, and Gordon ran right up after him. Buffy, he took a heck of a wuppin' from Gordon, but he didn't cry.

"Buffy kep' awful quiet rest of the afternoon, moped about the house like he'd swallowed a scrawny partridge. Wouldn't eat a single pea for supper. Just stared at his plate. But when I brought out the blueberry pie he plucked up courage, squared at Gordon, stuck out his lower lip and said, 'Didn't hurt.' After that he felt good enough to eat some dessert."

"Feisty kid, Cora," I say, heading for the door in earnest this time. "Takes after his grandpa. Now, I really must go. Keep warm, and don't worry about me in the storm. The Jeep'll get through."

"Oh, I'm not worried 'bout you, Kevun. I said to Gordon after we first met you, 'That man may be from Connecticut, but he's got the soul of a Mainer. Belongs here. Just like one of us.'

"I'll have Gordon bring Arvilla a jug of water to tide her over, soon as he finishes eatin'. You ought to be back by sundown."

I let myself out into the storm feeling toasty warm with Cora's cheer.

A stone chill entombs the Muir's upper West Side garret. The failing March light washes the tallow plaster a ghastly gray. A young woman sits and scrapes, thinning the cane with a scalpel for a soprano shawm reed clamped to the table before her. Strains of a renaissance band practicing Susato's *Danserye* drift from the tape deck. A key rattles in the lock and her husband enters. She lifts her narrow-set dark eyes. Her hands leave their work and slip beneath the blanket shrouding her slender frame.

"The fire's almost out, Vi."

Miriam's syrupy contralto seems to anesthetize him, allowing the message to penetrate without igniting his full fury. Villiers stands, hunched in the entry, and blows into his mealy hands.

"Nonsense. I loaded the bloody thing this morning."

Without removing his great coat, he swoops to the Godin like an arctic horned owl closing on a defenseless lemming. Crouching before the stove's filigreed iron cylinder, he pumps the grate shaker, curses and lifts the lid, releasing an acrid whiff of coal gas.

"Come, have a look at this, Miriam. The coal's gridlocked."

Miriam clutches the wool at her throat, rises and shuffles over to peer into the stove's black maw. Villiers prods the suspended anthracite with a poker, and the charge breaks up and clatters to the grate to join the few glowing cinders that remain there. A satisfying crackle of ignition follows a dusky puff of ash. He slams the lid and spins open the draft.

"It's time you learned how to run this stove, Miriam. Mind closely. Every six hours jiggle this lever until you see the coals glowing brightly in the window. Once a day, give it a full charge from that scuttle and draw off the ashes here."

"Yes, dear." Miriam slips back to her scraping. Twenty-six and not much bigger than the stove herself, she is an easy mark for her husband. In age, weight, bearing and station, Villiers outclasses her by a factor of two, but it is she who has kept the spark between

42

them alive these four years, mainly through compliance—irresistible to an upper-class Englishman.

Villiers, however, is insatiable, having sucked so long at her soul he has depleted her meager resources to supply his ego. Her voice—somehow still rich and resonant—is all that is left.

Miriam struggles to smile. "How was your day, love?"

"Dreadful, simply dreadful. Max called from London with the cheery news that Ormes can't get enough pear from Holland for the treble recorders, so they'll have to use sycamore. It's too soft. We can't sell a wooly sounding treble. I tried Mollenhauer and Hopf, but they can't supply the quantity we need. Just as well. I don't think much of their workmanship these days. What's for supper?"

"I'm sure you'll find a reliable firm. What about Korber? They put out a serviceable line of double reeds. Bennet, one of my students, has a Korber schalmai. Seems okay. 'Course, it's maple."

Villiers rubs his hands together. "Miriam, I don't like your students coming here. They should meet with you at a proper school—a public place. You're vulnerable here. God forbid, one of them tries to take advantage of you."

"We're having fish and chips, dear. It'll be ready in a half hour. I made coleslaw from scratch. Crispy, just the way you like it."

"Don't change the subject. I'm talking about your safety."

"You asked me about supper, Vi."

Villiers is crimson and shaking. "Stop that bloody scraping, Miriam. Stop it, this instant!" He seizes her by the shoulders and lifts her from the chair. The scalpel falls from her hand. He holds her scrawny ninety pounds aloft.

"Don't get impudent with me. I've a good mind to terminate your teaching altogether."

Villiers' jealousy is not without foundation. For the past three months Bennet and Miriam have been making more than music together. With the affair matured to the point of commitment, Miriam finds herself no longer afraid of Villiers. Her voice teases like an alto sax. "You sound like you'd like to terminate *me*."

"Listen, ducky. You'll do exactly as I say. Tomorrow, you'll see about a room at the university."

"I have lessons scheduled."

"Cancel them." Villiers sets her down, lifts the phone from its cradle and hands it to her.

"As you wish, dear."

Miriam calls off Bennet and her two other students without a hint of favoritism in her inflection and then sidles to the bar.

"Let me fix you an aperitif, Vi?"

Miriam pours Villiers a brandy and brings it to him, then busies herself in the kitchen while he sips and studies his instrument catalogs.

Minutes later, with supper in place, she calls him to the table. Villiers stumbles into the dining room, rubbing his eyes and yawning. "I'm all in, love. This rat race has worn me to a nubbin."

"Try some of my coleslaw. That'll perk you up."

"Aren't you going to have some?"

"Can't, darling. I'm allergic to horseradish, remember?"

"Mm. Too bad. It's delicious."

"Glad you like it. There's more fish in the oven."

"No thanks." He yawns again. "I think I'll toddle off. Don't forget to shake down the Godin before bed."

"Poor old sleepyhead. Sweet dreams, darling." She gives him a peck on the cheek and heads him toward the bedroom. "Every six hours. See, I remembered?"

"Good girl." Villiers' speech has become slurred. He reels and falls face down on the bed.

Perfect timing, she thinks. She returns to the living room, lifts the receiver and dials. "Bennet—he's sound asleep. Come quickly."

She hangs up and begins placing newspapers in a thick layer on the floor; first in the bathroom, then a swath down the hall to the stove in the studio. She shakes the grate, notes the level of the orange disc of embers in the hopper and adds just enough fresh coal to cover it. Returning to the bathroom, she fetches the hair dryer and props it on the marble coffee table she's dragged in front of the Godin. She hears a soft knock at the door, flies to it, draws the lock and falls into the arms of a slight, blond man with a square jaw.

"God, Bennet. I'm so scared. I don't mind the cremation; it's the quartering. Can't we put him in the furnace in the basement?" Bennet pushes her aside without answering. He has his shawm case with him.

"I hope you take students in the evening. The doorman looked at me strangely."

"Sometimes, sweetheart. Don't worry. He knows you're one of my regulars." She pauses to flash him a reassuring smile and then shudders. "Did you remember the wire saw?"

"Look, I know this is unpleasant, but we can't risk moving his body from the apartment, even in the freight elevator at night. The Godin can only accept one-foot chunks, so we've got our work cut out for us."

"Cripes, Bennet."

"And just what do you think this is all about?" His eyes flick focus about the room. "Do you have the garbage bags ready?"

"They're in the bathroom."

"Okay. Stuff this pillow into one." He hands her a plump cushion from the couch. "It'll seal better, and it won't take as long."

Bennet checks the bedroom. Villiers has rolled over on his back and is snoring. Miriam comes in with the poly-wrapped pillow. They had rehearsed their moves, even in the event that Villiers slept on his side or stomach, but he had made it easy for them.

Bennet nods and they jump him in concert. Miriam places the pillow over his head and straddles it. Bennet pins his arms and torso down. Villiers grunts and thrashes briefly. Though more than strong enough to free himself from them under normal circumstances, the six Seconal she'd slipped into his drink has weakened his defenses and clouded his brain, so that it takes only five minutes to snuff him out, but Bennet insists they keep the pillow in place a while longer, to be sure. Satisfied that he is dead, they drag Villiers to the bathtub.

Miriam falls back against the toilet. Her eyelids flutter and close. "Bennet, I can't."

"We've been all through this, and you agreed. It's the only safe way. Turn on the blow dryer." Bennet opens his instrument case and uncoils the saw. "We'll start with his head. It should just fit." Miriam staggers to her feet and treads the paper path to the Godin. She unscrews the draft wheel and aims the dryer at the opening, then plugs it in. From within the firebrick-lined cylinder a dull roar erupts that beats with the whine of the dryer. Moments later the cast iron exhaust elbow turns cherry red and then a bright orange. Miriam leaves her post, rushes to the toilet and vomits.

Bennet is all business. "Okay, Miriam. Let's try something. I think we can work the saw with your eyes closed. You take this end and pull when you feel me slack off." He hands her one of the rings and stretches the wire across Villiers' neck. "Now pull... rest...pull...rest...That's it."

Miriam begins to retch again, whooping dry heaves like a steam siren, but she swallows hard, closes her eyes and begins drawing the wire to her lover's commands. It takes only twenty strokes for the diamond dust-coated saw to sever the spine. After the fourth stroke Bennet starts the water in the tub to help mask the sound and rinse away the blood and bone-chips.

"I'll feed the stove. You just sit tight." Miriam keeps her eyes shut while Bennet stuffs the sack with Villiers' head and carries it to the waiting inferno. She hears the squeal of the dry iron hinge as the lid goes up, then the awful thud followed by the clap of the thin plate casting dropping onto its ground seat.

Bennet starts the tape and turns up the volume to drown out the crematory's dirge. It's the Bouree, with him playing lead reed. "Sounds better than I thought it would," he muses.

Miriam approaches from the hall, drawn and shaking, and slips into his arms. Together they wait, watching the color of the exhaust elbow gradually return to its former hue.

"I'm scared to death, Bennet. If we get caught, we'll both get locked up for life."

"Chin up, brave girl. Take a deep breath. The Godin's ready for its next morsel."

Miriam closes her eyes again and clings to him as they move back to the bathroom. Villiers' limbs, taken in halves, are easier to manage. His abdomen is another matter. By nine o'clock they have it worked into digestible chunks and flushed most of his vital fluids down the drain. The stench fatigues Miriam's olfactory sense before they reach his guts, and she becomes numb to the experience.

But not numb enough to open her eyes.

* * * * * *

Micah Gorman is a light sleeper. Ever since his escape from Auschwitz he has been on guard. At night, he insists on the bedroom window being open a crack, even in winter, so he can listen for threatening street sounds that might herald another search leading to his capture. He would be ready for them this time. Behind the suits in his closet rests his loaded Smith and Wesson.

The bedroom window of the Gormans' tenth floor Central Park West apartment faces the Hudson River, and the March breeze that night comes from the west. A police siren awakens Micah just after midnight. He lies in bed listening to its Gestapo-warble as it rises in pitch and intensity then fades to a minor key as the car recedes. Normally he would have dozed off again, but the smell in the bedroom keeps his adrenaline pumping.

The smell, unlike the usual burning butter fragrance of vehicle exhaust and garbage, is an odor he knows all too well: the putrid stench of incinerating human flesh.

"Mein Gott, Eva. They've found our people." He tugs at the sleeve of his wife's nightshirt.

"Go to sleep, Micah. You're in New York. The war is over. Twenty years, already, it's over. Take your Sominex."

"They're burning Jews again." He starts for the window.

"Micah, for God's sake. It's a vet incinerating the dogs he couldn't save. They do it at night when people are supposed to be asleep, when it won't bother anyone."

"It's *human* flesh, Jewish flesh. It's unmistakable." He throws the sash open wide and peers out over the sleepless city, gasping deep breaths. Nothing unusual catches his eye.

"Come to bed, Micah. You can research it in the morning. You'll put us both in the hospital with pneumonia, keeping that window open."

"Born and raised in Brooklyn, how the hell could you know what I'm smelling right now?"

Micah stumps to the phone in the hall and dials the eighty-fourth street precinct. After identifying himself, he blurts, "Someone's burning a Jew just west of here." He pauses. "How do I know? Listen, mister. I'm seventy-five. I survived the death camp at Auschwitz. I know the stench of cremation." He pauses again. "No, not animal flesh. And you've got no crematory in the city."

"Come to bed, Micah. Leave the police alone. God knows, they have enough to do without chasing Mengele's ghost."

* * * * * *

Just after three in the morning, insistent knocking awakens the doorman dozing on the settee inside the entrance to the Muir's brownstone. He drags himself to his feet and answers the door. A rookie police officer lets himself in and, without enthusiasm, begins his interrogation.

"Has there been any trouble with the heating system in your building tonight?"

"Not to my knowledge, sir. Why?"

"We're investigating a complaint about stack emissions in the neighborhood. Do any of the tenants in your building have heaters vented to the outside? Wood or coal stoves?"

"I wouldn't know; I've no occasion to enter the apartments, but the super could tell you. He'll be in at nine, if you'd care to stop by then."

"Have you seen anyone bringing in firewood or coal?"

"Sure. People often bring in wood during the winter. I think there are several apartments with fireplaces."

"How about coal?"

"Can't say as I noticed anyone bringing in coal, but stuff like that, in bags, is hard to tell from dog chow. Plenty of folks have dogs."

"Thanks for your help." The officer turns to leave but on his way out he remembers to inquire, "See anything suspicious coming in or going out from the building this evening?"

"No fuel, if that's what you mean."

"How about people? Any strangers?"

"Just the regular tenants and their friends and clients."

"Clients? Does anyone have a night practice in the building? A physician? A veterinarian, perhaps?"

"No, but there's a music teacher on the top floor that has pupils come for lessons, usually in the afternoon."

"You've been most helpful. Thank you." The officer turns to leave. Twisting the cast bronze Norwalk doorknob decorated with butterflies and tulips, he pushes open the figured oak door and vanishes into the almost sleeping city.

It's Christmas Eve 1947 in New Sterling, Connecticut. I'm alone in our garage, searching for mementos among my mother's trash a week after my father confined her to Fairfield Hills hospital for trying again to kill herself. In a brave last minute attempt to restore normalcy, Dad is out in the Olds, looking for a balsam to decorate. I'm their only child, Karcher, age ten, and I want nothing to do with Christmas.

The garage door is open and I'm shivering. I hear a distant heartbeat that matches mine, pulse for pulse. So compelling is the sound that I stop rummaging and move to the opening to listen. Only the occasional rumble of ice settling on Half Moon Pond masks the distant pounding.

As I stand there, straining to capture the sympathetic sound, I feel waves of warmth surging up my spine and radiating out to my shoulders, and realize I'm no longer shivering. In fact, I'm feeling strangely relieved. The chaos at home has finally subsided.

Whatever is making the noise draws me to the source and completely distracts me. Its measured thumping is relentless and absolutely reliable, in sharp contrast to the madness and inconsistency of my parents.

Jumping on my bike, I head north on Bald Hill. With only a light jacket, the bracing air has me pedaling hard to keep warm. At the corner of Lantern Ridge I stop to get a bearing. The pounding is a bit louder but still way off in the distance. At North Wilton Road I go left and continue for a mile or so until it intersects Route 35. There I stop again to listen. The thumping is louder still, and more detailed; at times, I can discern a steely hiss accompanying the beats as they rapidly crescendo to cannon fire. Thrilled and guided by the mysterious cacophony, I turn right on 35 and race downhill, fueled by pure adrenaline. When I reach Route 7, it becomes obvious that the thing resides just north of Wilton center, so I turn left and pump my bike uphill with all my might.

Atop the rise, just a quarter mile from Route 35, I see puffs of smoke belching from a tall pipe pointing skyward. I take a shallow right on Pimpewaug Road to get clear of traffic, and dismount in front of a dingy shanty bearing a faded sign printed in block letters: Gregory Brothers.

The door is padlocked, and a pie plate lamp over the entry casts an orange glow on the dooryard. Trying not to raise suspicion, I slip around the south side of the building and pick my way between abandoned tractors and rusting truck carcasses. In my excitement, I trip on a lump of cast iron lying almost obscured in the winter rye. Righting myself by stiff-arming a scaly John Deere fender, I lurch into a clearing.

There, standing in the stubble not twenty feet away is the apparition creating all the commotion. I'm transfixed. My watery eyes make it impossible to fully resolve the scene before me. The ground under my feet is quaking. Every organ in my body is shaking. The smell of freshly cut white pine, steam, oil and grease is overwhelming.

Blinking several times to clear my vision, I see that four people are attending a ferocious machine ripping boards from logs some twenty feet long with a large circular saw. As I watch, one man, caged in a stubby Bob Cat skid-steer, plucks a large pine from a pile and places it onto a rolling carriage. Another positions the log with a peavey then dogs it in place, while a third man stands near the end of the carriage rails, waiting to tail the boards as they come off the saw. The fourth person, a girl of about my age, dressed in denim hog washers, is pouring water from a pail into the engine's steaming hopper. I move closer.

The obstreperous engine commands my attention. Even when the saw is idle, its intake snorts and grunts like a contented sow while its exhaust marks time with bass drum thumps. Absent its load, the saw blade sighs like a night wind in the screens. Mesmerized, I watch the wide flat belt connecting the engine to the mill waving and wandering as I listen to its lacing ticking over the pulleys.

My reverie is short-lived when a log is fed to the saw's voracious teeth. Feeling the load, the engine erupts with cannon fire and tongues of flame. The skidding belt squeals in protest, and the saw peals a hoarse, mournful cry.

The girl leaves her post at the engine to attend the squealing belt, grabs a pump can and squirts some dressing on the inside of the lashing leather. The belt grips, falls silent, and exudes a pungent odor of rosin. Hastily returning to the engine, the girl makes a small adjustment to its mixture, tilting her head to better gauge the combustion response. Detecting a knock under full load, she cracks open a valve on the side of the hopper, to add a little hot water to the mixture. The knocking stops, and a deep V smile replaces her pout. Seeing her expression brighten, I pluck up courage and approach her.

"Where d'you learn all that stuff?"

Her frown returns. "Do I know you?"

"N…no. Sorry. I just stopped by to see what all the ruckus was about. I could hear this thing at home, about three miles away. It's really neat."

"Yeah, well, I gotta keep an eye on her so's no one gets hurt. If that saw chews on a chunk of iron imbedded in the log, I have to shut her down quick."

The girl turns back to her charge, preempting further conversation. I watch her give each main bearing grease cup a quarter turn, her small hands well clear of the slashing connecting rod, the plunging piston and the two whirling flywheels. She bends to peer into the cylinder oiler sight glass to count the drops and adjust the oil feed rate. Picking up a long-spout oil can, she tops up the cylinder oiler and dribbles a few drops onto the timing gears and exhaust valve cam. Satisfied, she leaves the huffing beast and heads for the Bob Cat idling at the log pile. The mill carriage is empty and the saw is spinning freely. Both sawyers are busy oiling the mill arbor and carriage transit pulley bearings.

Gaining confidence, I stroll over to the Bob Cat. The girl is clutching the loader's quivering cage, talking to the man inside.

Over the diesel's putter, I hear her say, "She's been awful good today, Daddy."

The man juts his chin toward the mill. "Couple more logs should do it." He squints as he scans his daughter's face. "You tired, Missy? 'Course you are."

"I'm not, either." Her lower lip protrudes as she backs away from the loader.

"We'll be done well 'fore dark," the father calls, waving off his young assistant. He revs up the Bob Cat and drives its forks under another log.

Without acknowledging my presence, his daughter returns to the engine, pulls a bandana from her back pocket and begins wiping condensate from the rim of the hopper while the men load the next log.

I take advantage of the lull and chance another approach. Moving just downwind of the thrashing engine and its attentive engineer, I'm temporarily immobilized by the aroma of girl sweat and steamed oil. A sharp warning delivered at close range kills my ecstasy.

"Back away from that belt, before you get hurt."

I move to my left but hold my distance from the engine. The girl takes a swipe at the brass nameplate on the side of the hopper, then turns to follow me with her enormous gray eyes.

Drawn by her small hand to the identification plaque, I lean in to read it. WITTE is stylistically blocked in large letters across the top. Below, it says Witte Engine Works, Kansas City, Mo. And at the bottom, in small font, punched into the soft brass, I learn that the engine develops twelve horsepower at 350 rpm and carries the serial number B42431.

"That's close enough!"

As if to emphasize the girl's warning, the engine fairly explodes, barking flames and shuddering fearfully as the saw starts howling. At close range, the song and fury is so intense that tears spurt from my eyes. The girl is all attention now, adjusting the mixture to compensate for the falling fuel level in the tank.

The first slab falls away, the log is turned to remove the remaining bark, and the squared timber is positioned for ripping a board. The sawyers move with choreographed precision, dancing to the downbeats of the Witte. Three boards cut clean, but part way through the fourth I hear a blunderbuss **"BANG!"** followed by a warbling scream from shrapnel whizzing just over my head. I feel a sharp pain in my right ear and move my hand there. Blood trickles down my wrist and I think I'm going to faint. The belt chirps and jumps its pulleys, flopping into a pile of oversized linguini. Both sawyers dive off the mill platform and crumple to their knees. With one twist of her wrist, the girl closes the needle valve, and the engine pants to a stop, accompanied by clunks from its Wico magneto and gurgling from the water boiling in its hopper.

I'm reeling, stumbling around in circles, holding my bleeding ear. The girl is focused on the mill and unaware of my injury.

The sawyers rise to inspect the damaged blade. "Look at this, Dana. Not one damn tooth left. It's shot to hell."

"Looks like it hit a grapple point, Cy. Thank God those teeth missed us; they must have sprayed way over Route 7 into the alders."

The girl's dad has bolted from the skid steer and is running toward her. "You all right, Missy?"

Only then does the girl notice me. "Yes, Daddy, but I think he's hurt." She gestures in my direction. Both rush to my side, arriving just in time to catch me as I pass out.

When I regain consciousness, I'm lying on my back on the ground. My face is wet and someone has placed a damp towel around my head. My ear is throbbing. Four faces are looking down at me.

I recognize the girl and her father right away. The two older men's faces look almost identical; one speaks. "You're damn lucky that tooth just winged you, young fella. Another couple inches and it would have put your eye out."

The other twin frowns and shakes his head. "What are you doing here, anyway? You could have been killed."

The girl is glaring at me. "I tried to warn him, but he wouldn't back off."

"Maybe he took a fancy to you, Witte," the girl's father said, smirking.

I struggle to speak, stammering through a throat full of phlegm. "I…I just h…had to see the engine."

A taut little woman appears and shoos the others to one side. She bends over me, removes the towel and begins bandaging my ear. "Poor kid, guess you got more than an earful of my brothers' sawmill—and on Christmas Eve."

My head is pounding. I try to make sense of what I've heard and seen. Directing my focus with difficulty to the girl's dad, I ask, "Didn't I hear you call your daughter Witte?"

"Yuh," he inhales.

"But that's the name of the engine; it's on the plaque."

"That's right. My wife Ida named her Arvilla after her great grandmother, but she took such a liking to that engine when she was just a midge, we changed her name to Witte and kept Arvilla as her middle name: Witte Arvilla Murch."

"Enough genealogy, Loring. The boy needs help." Ida is assisting me to sit up. "Feelin' better, deah?"

"Yes, thank you. I think I can stand now." I struggle to my feet and weave, trying to get my balance.

Ida steadies my arm. "You took quite a hit. Small wonder you're woozy."

Undeterred, Loring continues. "Every time we drive down from Maine to visit Ida's brothers, Witte runs down to the mill to watch that engine. She helps Dana care for it, like it's a pet. When the sawing's done for the day, she gives it a kerosene bath, oils the piston and positions its skirt flush with the back of the cylinder, then covers it with tarpaper and that Model A fender. " He gestures to a rusty piece of tin lying behind the engine.

"Normally, two locals help Dana and Cy run the mill, but today bein' a holiday, Witte and I helped run it. My daughter knows that engine better than any of us men."

"Loring!" Ida scowls at her husband then crooks her arm around my waist and starts me toward the Gregory homestead on the hillside across Pimpewaug Road. "It's almost three o'clock, young man. Your parents must be wonderin' where you are. You should call them." She pauses. "I'm sorry; I don't know your name."

"Karcher...Karcher Stickney. Listen, I gotta get my bike; it's by the shop."

"After you check in at home, Karcher." She keeps steering me toward the house. "When I heard that saw let go, I grabbed the first aid kit and headed for the mill quick as I could."

"Well, I sure appreciate it."

"You oughta rest a while before headin' out. You're welcome to have supper with us. I made slumgullion; there's plenty for all hands."

"That's very kind of you. To tell you the truth, I don't want to go home. My mom tried to kill herself again last week. They locked her up in Newtown. I don't want to help Dad decorate the tree."

"How dreadful. I'm so sorry."

"This time, when my nanny Bente refused to sleep with her, my mom went outside, naked in the night with her Stevens twenty-two and began plinking at the stars. They argued, and Mom turned the barrel on herself. Fortunately, Bente was able to wrestle the gun from her before she could pull the trigger. I saw the whole thing from my bedroom window. I just can't celebrate Christmas."

"Course you can't, poor deah." Ida wraps her arm around my shoulder and tugs me tight against her several times then opens the back door. "Come in, Karcher. I'm goin' to fix you a nice cup of chamomile."

Ida sits me at the kitchen table and prepares tea for us both. She settles into a chair opposite mine and fixes me with an expression of mournful sympathy. "You came all this way on Christmas Eve to see the Gregory's engine? I guess you know my daughter's fascinated with it too. It's almost as if it has magical powers."

"For me, it seems to have healing powers. My head is clear again, and my ear no longer throbs."

"It's the tea, deah."

I nod but know it's the engine's dependability and regularity that restores me.

The door latch rattles and the work crew files into the kitchen. Loring leads and is the first to speak. "Smells good, Ida."

The sawyers Cyrus and Dana look crestfallen as a pair of bare-eyed cockatoos and hardly say a word upon entering, but Witte is quick to assess the situation, and turns everyone's attention toward me. Burning me with pupils as obscure as coal, she says, "It was him. He comes out of the blue, and 'bang,' we're in trouble."

Loring colors up and smacks his lips noisily. "Zip it, Witte. You know he had nothin' to do with it."

"Wouldn't have been hit if he'd stayed back, like I told him."

Ida rises from her chair, shaking. "That's enough, you two. It's Christmas Eve and we have a guest." She turns toward me. "Go call your dad, Karcher. The phone's back there on the wall."

I duck out of the line of fire, pick up the handset and dial Woodward 6-9283. As expected, Dad is upset enough without me having to divulge the sawmill catastrophe or my injury. I promise to be home by dark.

Returning to the kitchen table, I watch Cy lift the cover off the casserole and sniff. "You ought a come down here more often, Ida. Dana's cooking's marginal."

Dana snatches the cover from his brother, picks up the ladle and is about to dip into the stew for a taste when Ida stays his hand.

"Don't you do it, Dana!"

Dana drops the utensil and backs away from the stove. The Gregory twins clear a path for Ida to bus the slumgullion to the table.

"Sit right down, all of you."

Ida's tasty supper is consumed with grateful grunting, clucking and smacking, reminiscent of the Witte engine's barnyard intake noises, and I find myself snickering at the resemblance.

My mirth is apparently not appreciated by the engine's namesake, who seems determined that I remain repentant and miserable. "Karcher...if that is your real name, what happened today is nothin' to laugh about. My uncles' sawmill is out a business. A new saw will cost over five hundred bucks. You think that's funny?"

Loring and Ida simultaneously rise from the table, but before they can admonish their daughter, I hastily excuse myself, thank Ida for supper and scoot out the back door. At this moment, my dad's displeasure and my missing mother couldn't be worse than Witte's rejection.

* * * * * *

I visited the Gregory Brothers several times over the coming years, always finding them in the shop, sharpening Locke reel mowers. I'd stand in the doorway watching the red sparks fly from the grindstone and wait until Dana had finished a pass. He'd look up with a knowing smile, leave his grinder and escort me out to where the Witte lay, cold and covered with tar paper and that rusty Model A fender. He'd unwrap the engine, free the magneto trip arm with a stick and start it with a backward heave on the timing side flywheel. The Witte always responded with that wondrous sound, sending plumes of smoke and tongues of flame skyward, beating time with my heart.

But each time I visited, I noticed the old sawmill lying there, abandoned, rusting and rotting in the tall grass, its toothless blade a grim reminder of the catastrophe I witnessed on Christmas Eve in 1947.

Old Orchard Beach, Maine, July 17, 1956. A rumble of thunder from the west woke me from my nap on the beach. The sky seethed sepia. Gulls screamed their warning as they wheeled overhead. Out at sea, lightning burned a dull red swath through the mist. I waited for the report, counting the seconds. One, two, three, four, five—"boom!" I nudged my girlfriend asleep on the sand. "Storm's coming. It's about a mile away. We better get back to the bungalow."

Witte stretched, groaning a lusty octave lower than her normal pitch. She sat up and swept her dusky silken hair from her eyes. "What time is it, deah?"

"Nearly six."

"Oh, m'gosh. I told Manny I'd run the lemonade stand tonight."

"On Saturday night?"

She frowned. "Now, look. I promised."

"Jeez, couldn't you call in sick or something?"

A loud clap of thunder terminated our argument. We streaked for Witte's barrack on Kinney Street behind Dave's Delicatessen where she worked, but a downpour caught us on East Grand, saving us the trouble of showering.

Witte was in a panic. Barely inside the door, she tore off her bathing suit right in front of me. I gasped and gaped, unable to speak. She yanked on her panties and jeans and wrestled a bulky, lavender sweater over her head without bothering with a bra, then shook out her sopping tresses and wound them in a towel, pulled on a white poncho, and dashed out into the storm, calling, "See yuh on the pier, Karcher. I'm off at ten."

I stood gazing out the door, dumbfounded and dripping. A flash of lightning froze Witte in a bounding pose as she turned the corner at a full gallop.

A wave of nausea swept over me. Feeling faint and starting to shake, I sank to sit on the edge of the bed and began talking to myself. *I'm going to be okay. She isn't abandoning me. She loves me. Calm down. It's all right.* After several deep breaths I began to feel better.

I dried and dressed then went around the room, straightening each misaligned object I came to, placing parallel her hairbrushes, combs and cosmetic tools on the dresser, smoothing the bedclothes, hanging the wet towels so their corners matched, adjusting the washbasin faucet handles to the same angle. I was feeling much better.

When the storm abated, I ventured forth. The air was saturated with the scent of honeysuckle in bloom. As I walked west along East Grand, the fading breeze loosened large droplets from the trees. The fir-planked boardwalk smelled like the deck of a schooner after the rain. In the clinging dampness, the lights on the pier took on an exaggerated luster. Still feeling uneasy, I climbed the ramp to the Dentzel carousel.

The organ sounded especially melancholy that night. Moisture pumped in by the storm had altered the tuning of the wooden trumpets. Their honking reminded me of a junior high school band rehearsing, trying so hard to please the teacher but never getting it quite right. *"Boo-Hoo,"* the organ cried. And so did I.

Composing myself with harsh words of criticism learned from my mother, *Don't be a damn fool. Pull yourself together,* I approached Manny's refreshment stand diagonally across the boardwalk. Witte was serving lemonade while raking her still damp tresses with a multi-pronged plastic fork. She winked and sucked in her cheeks to form a silent kiss while she kept her attention on a pack of thirsty preteens pressing her for service. Feeling the warm tickle of self-confidence returning, I waved and blew her a kiss before turning my attention to the carousel.

Vernon the operator was leaning against Jeff the giraffe as he rode the perimeter of the whirling platform, eyes focused at infinity. The ride was empty but the organ kept blaring, "Come Take a Trip in My Airship." As I approached, he acknowledged me with a barely perceptible nod and then swung between the standards like a monkey until he reached the center of the platform. He leapt to the control pad, grabbed the brake and held it until the ride stopped.

Seeing he was not busy, I plucked up courage to ask him if I might take a look inside the engine room. He glanced at the lighted office window above Noah's Ark where his boss kept an eye on the ride. Assured that the man was not at his desk, Vernon beckoned me to follow him.

I stepped aboard the wavering disc and wove my way past the carved cat with a fish in its mouth, the rabbit with floppy ears and several horses dressed for war until I reached a low door concealed in the side of the engine room. The organ music was deafening. We had to stoop to enter, and Vernon warned me to stay clear of the belts and gears if I wanted to stay inside when the ride was running. I did.

I gestured my thanks to Vernon and he ducked out. Wide-eyed, I began to study my surroundings. Creosoted timbers ran every which way. In one corner crouched a huge Century electric motor connected by a broad, flat belt to a large set of bevel gears. Overhead, support wires radiated from the center pole, and around the periphery of the top gallery ran broken segments of the ring gear that drove the crankshafts that lofted the horses.

The oak-veneered organ case with its roll cabinet doors open protruded from one wall of the multifaceted room, revealing the twin tracker mechanisms in operation. Tacked to the inside of the left door was a faded yellow tag. It read, Wurlitzer Military Band, Style 157. Below, were operating instructions for changing the music rolls, lubricating the bearings and gears, and cleaning paper chaff from the tracker screens. I stood, mesmerized, watching the perforated paper roll pass over the brass tracker bar, trying to discern which holes played the drums and which ones activated the pipe notes and registers.

Opposite the organ, under a menacing pair of gears, stood a cot covered with a moth-eaten army blanket where Vernon slept. I barely detected the odor of urine, so strong was the smell of creosote, grease and ozone.

My inspection was abruptly interrupted when the Century motor came to life with a groan that gradually rose in pitch until it became a whine. It snapped and flashed a magnesium-white arc when its shunt winding switched out. The belt creaked and squealed as the clutch engaged. Slowly, the center pole started to rotate. I ducked instinctively but kept my eyes on the wooden sweeps beginning to wheel above me. As the ride came up to speed, the belt's squealing subsided to a rhythmic slap. Whipped by the sweeps, the air in the engine room became delightfully breezy, distorting the organ's blare. Between each tune, I could hear faint cheering from children riding the wooden menagerie outside. A deep, satisfying purr emanated from the carousel's bevel drive gears. I thrilled to the furious pace of the machinery surrounding me that seemed to be putting on a private show just for my benefit.

Somewhere between the fourth and fifth ride, the door to the engine room opened and Vernon appeared, motioning for me to come out. He shouted something in my ear about a young lady outside looking for me.

Reluctantly, I emerged from my safe room where everything behaved with predictable precision. I glanced at my watch; it was almost ten fifteen. In my reverie, I lost track of time and, worse, I forgot about Witte.

She was at the canopy post where I usually stood to listen to the organ. Her brooding expression resembled the carved head of Medusa on the chariot in the third row. I worked my way around the chargers until I reached the perimeter of the carousel deck. The 157 paused after grinding out four identical verses of "Scatter-Brain" fox-trot.

"Figured where you were."

"Sorry, I was just…" Gesturing to the slim engineer in the orange shirt, I continued, "Vernon said it was okay to look inside and… Look, I know you're mad at me, but it's really neat in there. All the gears and belts. And you can see the guts of the organ. It's a Wurlitzer 157."

"What's the number 157 got to do with us?"

The organ began to play the waltz "Love is All" from the film *It's a Date*. It struck me that the 157 had a great deal to do with my feelings for Witte, though the association was not fully clear. Shouting above the blaring trumpets and crashing traps, I faced Witte with renewed confidence. "Come, I'll show you."

"Are you crazy?"

I stepped off the ride and approached her. "It's important to me, Witte. Please."

"It's too loud."

"Not so much inside, behind the organ. You'll be fine."

"I hardly think so."

"Come on,"

I grasped Witte's hand and gently towed her aboard the carousel, introduced her to my mentor and asked if I could show her the engine room. Vernon shrugged and urged us to get inside quickly because he had to start the ride.

Holding her ears, Witte stooped to clear the low doorway and followed me inside. The 157 paused again but its flat leather belt kept the crankshaft churning, pumping the bellows and pulling the music paper down with a mysterious thumping and flapping sound that convinced my wide-eyed girl to keep her hands firmly in place.

We heard a wooden knock as the forte register set and the swell shades on the front of the organ opened, revealing a latticework view of the already loaded ride. A ship's bell tolled once and the Century motor in the corner began to groan. Witte backed against the wall as far from the machinery as possible. She looked terrified. I was beaming.

The carousel started to turn. A split second later, the 157 drew all stops for the introduction to the "Beer Barrel Polka" played with stately deliberateness, finishing with a two-octave glissando. The forte register cancelled and the swell shades closed for the verse.

I looked at Witte with pride. She was braced and wincing, still holding her ears. The breeze from the whirling sweeps tugged her fine, long hair, drawing it over her left eye and cheek. I took her in my arms and tucked the errant skein behind her ear with my greasy hand. When I got through pawing her neck and cheek, she looked like a little kid who had fallen off her bicycle in the mud.

"W—we oughtn't stay h—here, Karcher. It's dangerous."

"Vernon said it was okay. Don't worry. I'll protect you." I rocked her in my embrace. "You see, this is my world. I feel safe here. These pounding, growling and grinding hunks of machinery are my friends."

"Yuh?" she inhaled.

The organ began playing the waltz "Chatterbox" from the musical *That's Right, You're Wrong*. I misted up at the yammering of its celesting violins and piccolos, squealing and wailing like a throng of two-year-olds.

"That organ oughta be tuned."

"For me, part of a carousel organ's charm is in the dissonance of neglect."

"Yes, well, I've had enough. This room's filthy, and you're filthy, too. Just look at you."

"Have you seen yourself lately?"

"I can just imagine. Look, it's nearly eleven." She started for the door but I grabbed her arm and pulled her to me. "You want to get hurt? The ride's going." She weakened her resistance a little. "Besides, I figured we'd do a little exploring here, if you know what I mean."

Witte looked up with a kittenish expression. "You're awful cute, even when you are dirty."

Still holding her, I plunged a soul kiss down her throat and edged her toward the cot. She swooned and we both nearly lost our balance. I felt her warm, unbridled breasts rolling under her sweater against my abdomen and her hot breath encircling my neck.

Reaching up, I unscrewed the solitary light bulb, plunging the engine room into near darkness. Only a flicker of colored lights from the revolving ride found its way through the cracks around the organ. Grotesque shadows of the center pole, of the sweeps and the gearing, fringed in changing colors, played around the room. The 157 was pounding "Ain't 'Cha Comin' Out." My jeans were already bulging.

Witte's calves struck the edge of the cot, jolting her out of her trance. "Whoa, deah. Where we goin'?"

"Stay here with me," I pleaded, pulling her gently down on the bed. I was starting to lose control but, surprisingly, it felt good this time.

The organ music with machinery accompaniment grew to a thunderous, beating roar, resonating with the pounding of my heart. Above us, the gears gnashed their teeth as they slowly turned, occasionally dropping blobs of black grease that narrowly missed our writhing bodies.

Witte turned hot and sweaty as I stroked her, moaning softly as she twisted on her back, hands overhead, palms up, as if surrendering to a raging fever. I straddled her and slowly lowered myself until our bodies melted.

Overwhelmed with passion, Witte was racked by a seismic orgasm. The contraction started in her neck, sending her head to the side with a jerk. Her fingers fanned and shot rigid. Lying on top of her, I could feel the powerful pressure wave as it passed down through every muscle in her body. When the paroxysm reached her back, she drove her breasts into my solar plexus. Her abdomen became hard as a boulder. Her hips thrust, lofting me where it counted and forcing an involuntary groan from my throat. Finally, her legs twitched as the spasm reached her thighs. I thought she was about to deliver a baby.

"Are you all right?"

Sweat beaded up on her forehead. She gasped several breaths, tossed her head from side to side, clenched her fists and let out a bestial groan from somewhere deep inside. Then she fell limp. I waited anxiously for her to speak.

Sighs were all I heard for the first minute or two. I could see that she wanted to reassure me, but the words just would not form. As her skin cooled, the sweetest smile formed on her lips. She struggled then to answer me.

"Karcher, you put me in paradise."

The 157 started hammering out "It's Better with a Union Man." Mental pictures started to roll, frame after frame, through my confused brain: ungoverned engines running away, safety valves shooting plumes of steam, locomotives bearing down on me as I sat between the rails, crippled and unable to move.

"Your turn," came a little voice in my ear. I felt a small hand slide down my chest until it fetched up on the root of the matter. I curled up with pleasure. Another little hand was busy unbuttoning my shirt, unlacing my belt, and gradually drawing down my zipper. I lay back, closed my eyes and counted all sixty-five teeth of that zipper.

When I opened my eyes, Witte was kneeling alongside, bending over me. Her long hair tickled my chest as she moved. Throwing a leg over me, she leaned forward and dragged her hair across my face until she went out of focus. I felt her tongue caress my open lips then my teeth. Her kisses extended outward in swirls to encompass my chin, nose and forehead, interrupted only by sighs. As she nibbled my ears, she whispered, "Now, I've got 'cha where I want 'cha."

The 157 reached the end of its repertoire with a pair of clunks separated by a brief whir as the music drive cam rolled over, shifting the feed to the other roll and commencing to rewind the roll that had just finished playing. Seconds later, it commanded, "We Must Be Vigilant" ("American Patrol" plagiarized for dancing), prompting me to reach for the pack of XXXX condoms in my pocket. My hands shaking, I fumbled trying to open the little plastic condom case, spilling the cool liquid that preserved the delicate fish membrane. (I wanted to strangle Julius E. Schmitt for interrupting our lovemaking.) Witte giggled.

I was teetering on the brink of ecstasy when I felt Witte start to go rigid again. She began to writhe as another spasm worked its way down her fragrant body. When it reached her waist and her hips kicked, I could hold back no longer. Together, we howled our sweet agony into the thundering shadows.

The 157 finished the fourth verse of Walt Disney's "It's an Actor's Life for Me," dumped its vacuum and began to rewind.

The ride had stopped. Only the pounding of our hearts and the steady "ticka-tacka, ticka-tacka, ticka-tacka" of the organ's worn pump rods disturbed the silence in the engine room.

Witte glanced at my watch. "Gosh, deah, it's nearly twelve."

Feeling severely debilitated, I struggled to elevate myself to a seated position on the edge of the cot. The lower half of my body just wasn't there. Somehow we managed to get each other dressed. Witte, looking like she had just emerged from a cement mixer, commented thickly, "You 'bout drowned me, Karcher."

Clutching each other for support, we stumbled over to the light. Hearing the door latch click, I quickly screwed in the bulb. The door creaked open and Vernon entered, averting his eyes as he moved about. He switched off the organ's cranking motor and killed the power to the Century then exited, leaving the door open behind him.

Nodding our thanks to Vernon, we wobbled into the night, arm in arm, past the darkened rides, along the dampened boardwalk and down East Grand to the bungalow. Witte looked radiant and delightfully spent as she fell against the door and began twisting her key in the lock.

One look in the mirror was all it took. We laughed ourselves silly at the sight of our tousled hair, besmirched faces and rumpled clothing. Witte tore off her clothes and dashed for the bathroom. "I get the shower first."

"Oh, no, you don't," I said, hopping after her on one leg, trying to extricate myself from my sticky jeans. Stubborn and giddy, we showered together, taking turns washing each other. Witte's dainty, drenched form and the feel of her body as I slid my hands over her soapy curves made my insides crawl with desire. She looked so tiny and vulnerable with her hair almost obscuring her face and streaming over her breasts.

We dried each other with unusual interest, taking much longer than necessary, and I received a few too many compliments cooed from little pursed lips.

"I'm not through with you yet," I said, scooping her up and carrying her, squealing and kicking, into the bedroom. I plopped her on the bed, rolled her onto her back and leaped upon her, spilling her damp, fine hair across the pillow like a hurricane sky. She giggled and wriggled under me as I attempted to nibble her nose and kiss her neck. But when my hand cupped her breast, her struggling and laughter subsided. Fixing her eyes on mine with her eyebrows steeply inclined, she sighed and said, "Nobody run me good as you."

Late for work, she'd driven straight to the top deck of the garage, knowing the lower levels would be filled, and parked sloppily in a large vacant bay farthest from the elevator. Before she could get the key out of the ignition, a surprisingly seedy late-model BMW pulled alongside and parked dead center in the next space, so close she couldn't open the long driver's door on her Cougar more than a crack. Its driver was gone by the time she'd finished crawling over the console, hooking the heel of her pump on the floor shifter and snagging a nylon on the power seat's joy stick in her rush to exit the right door. There were five empty spaces to the right of the crooked Cougar and three to the left of the pitted pewter compact car crowding it.

"Shit!" spat the woman into the concrete womb of stillborn sedans and crouching coupes. She stiff-armed the door and bent to smooth her suit skirt then straightened with a toss of her bangs. "Fucking BMW yuppies think they own the world!" Snatching her attaché case, she clicked off the fifty paces to the elevator.

Pattin Stickney reached her desk from the rear hall of the bank at nine ten, her boss Ken Larkin right behind her.

"Who owns a beatup BMW in the building, Ken?" she said without looking up from straightening the mess of forms on her desk. "You know what that H.C. did? Parked nearly on top of me. Ripped my L'eggs going over the console."

"Sounds kinky. No one with the initials H.C. that I know of. Bob Brenner the dentist has a red 318i, but he wouldn't be at work yet."

Pattin shot Ken a scowl. "H.C. is an abbreviation for horse cock, wiseass. Besides, it was a ratty silver. If I catch that arrogant SOB, I'll pull his little pink tie."

"I hope your offender isn't a woman."

"Have you ever seen a woman driving a BMW?"

"Well, come to think of it, no."

Pattin dropped into her chair and dismissed Ken with a jut of her chin. She turned toward a small queue of customers waiting to open accounts or to rail at the bank for alleged errors, most of which were theirs. First in line stood a tidy, fiftieth-percentile male in his mid-thirties, perhaps ten years older than herself. "May I help you?" she called, forcing a smile.

The square-jawed man muttered as he approached. Strings of pasty saliva bridged his thin lips and tore away as he spoke. "I chose this bank because it promised prompt posting of my deposits and rapid check clearing."

"Won't you sit down, Mr.—?"

"Warner. Giles Warner."

"Mr. Warner, how may I be of help?"

"Dirigo Northern is a phony," he began, the facing chair barely supporting his rigid, intrusive torso. "Lots of hype and no substance."

Pattin leaned back in her chair to avoid the next salvo of saliva. "Mr. Warner, please. Get to the point."

Giles moved closer. "Your computers can't keep up. I deposited my paycheck in your Timeless Teller after hours yesterday and tried to draw out two hundred in cash. The damn robot said I had insufficient funds. I'd just fed the thing eleven hundred and fifty dollars!"

"What time was it when you made your transaction, Mr. Warner?"

"Three forty-five. Why?"

"The computer goes off line for a half hour between three thirty and four, to process the day's backlog of transactions. During its break it cannot give cash. You just happened to catch it napping."

"Precisely my point." The spittle was now flying. "It can't keep up, and instead of explaining its inadequacy, it prints an erroneous message: INSUFFICIENT FUNDS! Do you know how that makes me feel, Ms. Stickney?" Giles was flushed and shaking. "Like kicking the crap out of the stainless moron. Twenty-four hour banking, indeed!

"Well, I fixed your Timeless Teller this time. I fed it a credit card-sized sheet of lead. Do you know what it printed after that morsel, Ms. Stickney?" He paused and thrust his face across her desk. "THANK YOU!"

Pattin dodged his spittle's new trajectory. Her smile came easier now. "So this has happened to you more than once?"

"Four times in the past two months. And just last week when I was in Rockland, I tried to withdraw funds from my account at the Yankee Four robot outside Deering Savings. It didn't even recognize my card! But the one at Northeastern Bank across the street did. What kind of a network are you running here?"

"We're not running the network, Mr. Warner. We just subscribe to the service. Some banks in the network choose not to communicate electronically with others out of town. That's their choice."

"Then why don't they post a notice to that effect? I'll tell you why. Because they're afraid they'll lose business. I went inside and told the Deering teller that they'll lose more business by angering people than by being forthright. They lost my business, and so now have you, Ms. Stickney." Giles collapsed in his chair, hyperventilating.

"Are you all right, Mr. Warner?"

A smile broke over his chiseled face. "I'm here to close out my accounts." He beamed triumphantly between gasps.

"I'm sorry Dirigo Northern and the Yankee Four network didn't live up to your expectations, Mr. Warner. I'll get your records." Pattin withdrew to the files across the room. She had the skin-crawling sensation that Giles watched her. When she returned with his folder, she busied herself leafing through his account forms, avoiding eye contact. "I see you have a CD, a regular savings and a checking account. Do you wish to terminate all three? There'll be a penalty for closing out your CD."

"That's what I said: close them out, all of them." He threw two passbooks on her desk. "I'll take my business to an honest institution."

"As you wish. Do you want cash or a teller's check, Mr. Warner?" Pattin's jaw was setting up and her speech was becoming clipped.

"Cash," he said peremptorily.

"I'll just be a minute." Pattin rose, buzzed herself through the teller's gate and began conferring with a woman at one of the terminals. Giles saw her sputtering and shaking her head. The teller looked sympathetic.

Ten minutes later, Pattin burst through the gate with a fist full of bills. "I know I don't have to tell you how frustrating it is to cope with a computer's moods, Mr. Warner." She fixed her huge gray eyes on him. "We just changed the CD account numbers to simplify storage and the mainframe lost your cross reference. I'm sorry for the delay."

"Computers don't lose data, Ms. Stickney. People perpetrate computer errors through inattention or stupidity, the same way they cause auto insurance rates to rise by failing to signal a turn or by parking discourteously. Why, just this morning some bitch left her car cater-corner in the garage, taking up almost two spaces. I'll probably have another ding in my door. And, of course, she'll be gone."

Pattin's eyes narrowed, the new bills crackled in her clenched fist, and the color went out of her cheeks. "You don't just by chance happen to own a silver BMW parked on the top deck of this garage?"

"As a matter of fact, I do. It's a 325i, parked next to that broad's canted Cougar. Why?"

Pattin raised herself to her maximum height without leaving her chair. "That *broad*, sir, is me! And I think I'm beginning to fathom this little charade. Let's call it 'Everybody's out of Step but Giles Warner.' I've a good mind to report your lead leavings to my boss and have you arrested for tampering. Now, take your money and get out of here before I lose my temper."

"I'd say you already have, Ms. Stickney." Giles was beaming. He left the money on the desk between them. "I've never been so deliciously rebuked by a woman in my life. I'm glad I met you."

72

His gaze dropped to his lap, and a tinge of rose brushed his cheeks. "I guess I've blown it, haven't I?"

"I'd say you've succeeded in mucking up my morning, if that was your intention." Pattin glanced over Giles' shoulder at her lengthening line of fidgeting customers. "And now I must ask you to leave so I can take care of these other people who have been waiting for nearly half an hour." She stood and held out the bills to him.

Giles remained seated and did not take the money. "You know, I think I've misjudged Dirigo Northern's integrity. If you are at all typical of its management, perhaps I could tolerate the inconvenience of banking here a while longer."

"Now, look, Mr. Warner. This has gone far enough. I have work to do, and so must you. I'm sure you can find another bank that will be more solicitous of your wishes."

"No, really. I've changed my mind. I want to keep my money here. Can you reopen my accounts?"

Pattin drew a deep breath, which did not go unnoticed, exhaled a protracted sigh and slumped into her chair. "You won't be satisfied until I'm carted away in a straitjacket, will you? Okay. Give me a minute to deflect these people to my senior officer." She rose and sidled away from her desk, turning away from him only when she'd gained the corridor.

Normally, Pattin would have turned over such an insatiable customer to Ken; he was good at defusing the difficult cases. But something stopped her. Warner was a challenge, and she seemed to be winning.

There was a confident lunge to her gait on the return trip. Ken had been most understanding and more than a little playful. "So, I was right," he'd said. "You did enjoy your tumble over the console."

"I prefer to exit by the driver's door," she'd said, but he could see she was blushing.

Pattin settled in her chair, leaned across her desk and presented a sheaf of papers. "Mr. Warner, I'm afraid you'll have to fill out these forms again." Her voice was controlled with an earthy profundity.

"Please call me Giles," he said, and began scribbling on the CD form. He paused, pen in midair. "Listen, I want to apologize for my rudeness. This has been a difficult transition for me." He put his pen down. "I moved to Maine last fall to escape the callous gold coasters. They call Fairfield County, where I lived, the boot of Connecticut, because of its shape. The shoe fits, if you know what I mean."

"What made you think things were different down east, Mr. ......Giles?"

"Oh, you know Maine's reputation for no nonsense, honesty and forthrightness. It's written all over Muskie's face on TV."

"I'm sure Mr. Muskie would be the first to admit that TV has spoiled the spirit of his people by showing them the luxuries that can be attained by pushing and shoving. The world is growing smaller. Why, we've even learned how to dance without touching."

Giles brightened. "You sound just like Muskie. I guess the media hasn't corrupted your morals. What I'm trying to say is, you're what I had in mind when I came up here. I mean, you represent the Maine I believed in."

Embarrassed, Giles bent to the task before him. His pen moved unsteadily under Pattin's glare. When he'd finished, he watched her moonstone tipped, tapered fingers drag the forms from his grasp.

"I'll have the teller cut you new passbooks. I won't take more than a couple minutes. I promise."

Giles watched Pattin repeat her trot to the terminal and back. She moved deliberately this time with well-oiled precision, hips swaying as she minced. Gone was her ragged gait, the jerky gestures. She led with her chest instead of her brow. At the teller a simper replaced her former scowl, and she gestured with her eyes several times in his direction.

Pattin did not resume her seat upon returning. She handed the passbooks across the desk with her left hand and extended her right to Giles. "I'm glad you decided to stay with Dirigo Northern, Giles. Have a nice day."

When Giles took her hand, they both knew it was more than a friendly farewell. "You've been so kind," he said with all the control he could muster, "that I'd like to return the courtesy. Let me take you to lunch?"

"You may have to, if we can't get our cars apart." Both laughed uncomfortably. "I'll tell you what," she said. "I usually grab a sandwich around the corner at Vi's. I'll meet you there at noon."

Giles tried to control his excitement, but his voice broke like an adolescent. "Sure," he squawked in a falsetto. "That'd be fine."

"Until noon, then." She smiled and turned her attention to her next client. "May I help you?" she called impersonally. Her change in tone made Giles feel special as he headed for the door.

* * * * * *

Giles knew about Vi's, a hole-in-the-wall luncheonette he'd assiduously avoided for its assumed working-class fare that he considered unpalatable. Against his better judgment, he opened the door. It was exactly noon. The place was packed. He peered into the rancid pall of cigarette smoke and swallowed hard to suppress a gag. A wiry woman of fifty was single-handedly flipping burgers, fanning the toasters, sloshing soup, busing plates, setting places at the tables and processing five or six conversations at once.

"She's over here," came a scratchy down east drawl over the din. Astonished, Giles noticed the woman was addressing him and nodding to the far end of the counter. He worked his way through a throng of linemen standing, swilling coffee. There wasn't a seat in the house. Pattin was occupying the last stool, wolfing a turkey salad sandwich.

"Sorry about this," she said over her shoulder when she'd cleared her mouth. "Just holler what you want at Vi when she gets within range."

Giles stared vacantly at the greasy plastic menu letters over the grill. "I'll just have coffee, maybe a muffin," he said meekly.

"You gotta speak up, Giles," Pattin encouraged, but there was no need.

"What kinda muffin, mister?" Vi already had the coffee beaker in hand.

"Do you have blueberry?"

"Course not! Corn or soda?"

Giles leaned over Pattin, trying to project his order to his moving target without calling attention to himself. "Corn will be fine."

"Toasted, deah?" called Vi without looking up from the sink where she was plunging glasses.

"Yes, thank you."

"Sure that's all you want?" Pattin asked, passing his mug of mud over her shoulder.

"This isn't quite what I had in mind for our luncheon," Giles said, choking down his crumbly cornmeal. He handed a fiver across the counter.

"She's already paid. Yours is eighty-nine cents."

Giles looked like he was going to cry. He put the change in his pocket and turned to leave. Pattin caught up with him outside, where he was heaving deep breaths and quietly cursing.

"You weren't supposed to do that," he sputtered, looking at Vi's restaurant license just inside the front window that listed the diner's capacity as twenty persons. "This place should be condemned. I counted thirty-five sweaty slobs in there, not including us. And the grill is filthy." The chalky gel had returned to his lips, and his face was ashen. "They have no right permitting such squalor, especially in this part of town." His eyes flicked focus several times before fixing on Pattin. "Those Board of Health bastards don't know what real indigestion is." He paused to belch. "Wait'll they get a taste of the suit I'm going to drop on them!"

"Giles, I'm really sorry." Pattin's long face, steeply raked eyebrows and tiny pout were so distracting that he couldn't finish his tirade.

"Have dinner with me tonight. No strings, just dinner. I pick the place. Okay?"

"I don't know, Giles. What if the bread is cold? Or the butter's too hard? You'll go to pieces."

"Not where we're going. I've eaten at this place so often, the maître d' and I are on a first name basis. I'll pick you up at seven." He caught a whiff of her patchouli. "Oh, I almost forgot to tell you. You left a window open on your car. I couldn't get in to close it."

"You need a key, deah. They're power windows. But thanks for trying." She began shuffling a serpentine path toward the bank, head lowered, deep in thought. At the door she stopped and turned to him. Her eyes said what he wanted to hear before she spoke. "My flat is on the hill, just below the observatory. Number twelve Monument Street. Top floor. Seven o'clock." She touched her temple. It was an almost subliminal salute, but one Giles would remember. Then she was gone.

* * * * * *

By six a fog had enshrouded all but Munjoy Hill, which peeked above the gossamer blanket like a naughty kitten. Portland was settling down for the night. Giles walked the docks anxiously, killing time. His driven life left little room for chasing women, and the few relationships he'd started in Connecticut had ended quickly. Pattin was his first date with a Mainer, and that made him especially uneasy, since he'd invested so much time and effort qualifying for the Maine bar, relocating and adjusting to his new utopia. She was not the prettiest girl – too skinny and a trifle knock-kneed, he thought, and there was always a storm brewing in her narrow-set eyes of northern gray – yet he felt drawn to her.

The city was engulfed in cloud by the time Giles rang the bell at number twelve Monument. Seven on the dot. In his zeal, he drove the button beyond its stop and caught it on the bezel. While he was trying frantically to extricate the plunger, the door opened revealing Pattin, laced into a dirndl, standing in the hall, arms akimbo, scowling. "You trying to wake the whole neighborhood, Giles?" She brushed past him, trailing her hypnotic musk, hooked a long oval fingernail under the button and popped it free before descending the stoop stairs. "You look spiffy tonight," she said as he held the right door of the battered BMW open for her. Pattin hesitated then slid smoothly into the leather bucket. "I don't suppose you're taking me to Vi's," she teased.

"How about Fagan's Ferry?"

"Long as you don't get obstreperous and rock the boat."

Fagan's Ferry restaurant was bridged to the pier parking lot by a canopied gang plank. The lot was gated with a spastic semaphore that, unbeknown to Pattin, was on Giles' shit list. A Lincoln Continental in front of them stopped at the gate. The driver pulled a ticket from the machine, the heavy beam lifted and the car started to drive through. Pattin sensed that something was wrong when she heard Giles hissing next to her. But before she could get a word out, he'd pulled up to the Continental's rear bumper, his engine revving, clutch slipping, yanked a ticket and shot ahead before the impersonal slug had time to reset. The beam descended and karate-chopped the BMW's cowl with a deafening thud then slid up the face of the windshield and scraped back along half the roof before it lifted. Even Giles ducked as the intrusive timber passed over them. The parking attendant at the exit booth fifty feet to the south burst from his cubicle when he heard the boom, and ran toward them, waving frantically. Giles ignored him and sedately drove to an empty spot near the ramp.

"You all right, mister?" the kid shouted as Giles got out to inspect the damage. Giles pretended not to hear him. Pattin perched, drawn and still as a long-eared owl.

"May I see your ticket?" said the boy with mild authority, now at Giles' elbow.

"How dare you ask for my ticket, young man, at a time like this? Your gate practically totaled my car, and you want to see my ticket? Look at this!" He gestured to the car's rippled roof. "I'm sure my insurance company won't take *this* lying down."

"I'm terribly sorry, sir, but I must see your ticket. See, some of these big shots try to run the gate, as if they own the place." The boy looked so innocent and unsure of his position that Giles softened and dug in his pocket for the ticket.

"I'm not one of your Cadillac clientele." Giles handed over the tiny orange scrap of card. The boy gave it back and slunk away in silence.

Giles already had the parking lot owner's name listed in his notebook, having contemplated for several months an attack on the semaphore, but until now he'd never had the right audience. He circled the car slowly, assessing the damage at leisure. It appeared to Pattin that he was relishing his findings: a telephone pole-sized trough across the cowl, the twisted remains of the wipers, the windshield scratches, and the gouges on the roof streaked with creosote—damage carefully calculated, she thought, to cop a convincing settlement from the owner's insurance without crippling his BMW. When Giles reached her side, Pattin flung open the door, stood and spat the mouthful of saliva she'd worked up, forcefully in his face.

"We could have shared that under different circumstances." She was crimson and shaking. "Now you know how I felt this morning sitting in your line of fire, Mr. Sicko Yuppie!" Giles had his initialed Irish linen handkerchief out and was mopping himself as best he could. "I know better than to get involved with a BMW owner. Why didn't I listen to myself?" Seeing that he wanted to say something, she lunged at him. "Oh, no, buster. I'm far from finished with you." Giles backed against a piling in horror. "I should save my breath and just shove you into that slip, you prissy bastard!"

Pattin panted in place for a moment before she resumed. "Know what your trouble is, fella? You don't know how to effectively express anger. So you tilt at windmills, slash at the formidable gates of evil with your teensy sword. Sure, there's a lot of injustice out there, even in Maine. But you're not smart enough to put your efforts where they'll do some good. Just look at that car of yours." She gestured behind her. "It's a testament to your impotency. Twenty-seven grand and beat to hell in one year by a schnook that parades his futility all over town. You should be ashamed of yourself. What woman would want to spend time with a man proud to be a mouse? I know my way home. And please, patronize another officer next time you bank at Dirigo Northern." Pattin snapped an about face, clattered up to speed and disappeared into the mist.

Things were no different in Maine after all, Giles reflected.

Snapshot

How presumptuous: A mechanical engineer subsisting on a literary diet of *Model Airplane News, Sports Cars Illustrated* and *Cycle World,* inviting himself to the first meeting of recent graduates from Yale University's creative writing class and bringing a sample of his scribbling. What chutzpah!

Just the opposite, actually. My emotional barometer having about hit bottom, this reckless recipe whet my appetite for rejection. Having flogged myself for a week and endured nonstop sympathy from my well-meaning wife, it was time to seek outside punishment to validate my worthlessness.

I confess I had encouragement from my wife's close friend and facilitator of the writer's group, Peg, a portly but entirely feminine Van de Graaff generator whose pate continuously discharges a shower of invisible sparks, a surfeit of cephalic activity largely wasted on a left-brained researcher like myself. Fortunately, Peg's syrupy solace, delivered in several telephone installments, had mesmerized me before I confronted her formidable word puzzle, *Point Blank.* What few faculties I had left vanished after the third attempt to read it, and in desperation—the meeting just days away—I turned to my wife for a translation.

"Oh, this is really clever," she said confidently. "Look, she's disguised the homilies by rewriting them in polysyllabic language."

"Okay, but what are those words without apparent context, plopped in caps between bits of dialogue?"

"Gee, I don't know. Hey, look at this. She's laid a musical score right in the middle of the text on page six. Weird." She thinks a moment. "I guess you'll have to ask Peg what she means by all this."

I did, and got a lecture on metafiction, whatever that is. I was told the piece was an etude for writers, intentionally obscure and definitely not for readers. That left me out on two counts. I couldn't even call myself a reader.

But by then I had used up a box of Kleenex scrawling six pages of emotional enginese for my initiation into the club, the catharsis having restored my ego to a point where I could ignore without guilt that which I could not understand. Upon reflection, my little sketch made so much sense that I was elevated to offer my services as chauffeur for the evening, and found myself ferrying four of the seven classmates to the Toad Hall of Devon Point.

* * * * * *

We arrive at seven-thirty on a balmy evening in June. The set is *Wind in the Willows* but the play is *Thirtysomething*. Burt comes with the set and plays Toad to a tee, rolling his benevolent brown eyes to direct our attention to each facet of his spacious, modern manor, the tragic bachelor with too much to share with too few. My eyes mist, but jealousy blocks the tears. Relief comes when the instant hot water tap produces tepid tea and there is no kettle to boil water in and we have to nuke our cups in the microwave. Burt graciously tolerates our amusement and invites us back for the grand tour at our next meeting.

The set soon shrinks to the kitchen table, and hidden agendas begin to float freely beneath it. I scan my opponents for a glimmer of acceptance. Their attention seems focused elsewhere: on each other, on the ambiance of Toad Hall, on their work to be presented.

Peg places a tray of chocolate-covered strawberries she's brought on the table and takes her place diagonally across from me. "Let's decide on a time to stop, because we have enough material here to fuel an all-nighter. How about ten o'clock?" There's a murmur of agreement.

A brief discussion follows about who should go first, and Burt is chosen to read his short story, "The Agency," involving a proud but destitute mother and her two girls who must accept welfare from a Catholic charity. He reads quickly, his glottis clipping, his capacious jaw masticating, his delivery a near monotone appropriate for this third-person, black-and-white video view of the woman's predicament. Most say the piece came off well, and Peg deems it worthy of publication. But the pert and available brunette newspaperwoman across from him takes issue with his punctuation, especially the absence of quotation marks around the dialogue.

"My editor would never allow the piece to stand without quotes." Lori is eyeballing Burt beneath a shock of raven bristles that could only have stood that erect in Peg's static field above and just to her right. He seems flustered for a moment but quickly regains his composure, careful not to reveal a hint of defensiveness.

After a short break, at the end of which about half the strawberries and most of a liter of Chablis had been consumed, Peg reads from a short story she's started but hasn't the courage to finish due to the painful memories it evokes—and not, thankfully, from *Point Blank*. This gives Burt a chance to retaliate.

"You always manage to work in a vacuum cleaner somewhere, Peg."

"Well, if Kevin can write engines into all his stories (my wife had apparently tipped her off), I can push a vacuum around in mine." I try not to flinch.

Chet shows up and I make room for him at my left. Physically, Chet could have been me twenty years earlier: pensive, slender and sensitive. But he steps out of my shoes when he removes his and works his bare toes into the plush pastel carpet beside my chair, displaying a confidence I lacked at his age to luxuriate in the deep pile and share his scent with us. Poor Chet is immediately attacked for not bringing a manuscript and has to defend himself. He succeeds in deflecting our focus to the palatial surroundings and closes by deprecating his meager four-room apartment.

The conversation drifts back to Peg's three-page teaser, and several ask her to reveal the plot. She firmly declines, promising to subject us to the balance of the thirty-odd pages at a future meeting. Groans all around.

"Who's next?" Peg pauses. We all look at our hands. "Kevin's brought us an excerpt from his novel, *The Aberration*. Why don't we take ten minutes to read it and then regroup?" Reluctantly, I pass out the copies. I begin pacing the whitewashed rooms, trying to find some artifact or construction detail to absorb my attention from the awful scrutiny. Nothing works, not even the art deco pinball machine, an anachronism in the stark exercise room that would ordinarily capture my imagination. I express appreciation to Burt who is following close behind me, having quit trying to decipher my enginese after rereading the first sentence three times. But what worries me more is the whispering among those still reading. As I wander at a polite distance, I can't quite catch their words, but their expressions make my stomach churn. When I can stand it no longer, I take my place at the table and try not to look at anyone.

Peg opens with, "I think it would help if you'd read it aloud, Kevin." With almost no saliva left, I begin to clatter feebly at a delirious pace, hardly pausing for breath. My heroine Witte's Maine dialect sounds unconvincing, and I garble the engine noises in my embarrassment.

There's a moment of relief when single Susan joins us. I stop to read her sensual lips curling with pleasure as her husky voice rolls on about her hectic schedule raising kids and holding down a job. Peg brings her up to date, and I resume with more conviction. Finally, it's over. The silence is unbearable.

"Well?" I say, still not looking up.

Peg inquires politely as to my intended readership. I tell her I wrote it for the antique engine collectors who I knew would enjoy it, adding, "But I'd hoped it would speak to others as well."

Howls of protest erupted from all points around the table, crushing out my last coal of confidence. The gist of their clamor was clear. I'd snowed them with technical terms so thickly settled and incomprehensible as to discourage *any* reader not conversant with tired iron.

After another protracted silence, the eyes with the pony tail directly across from me pipes up. "I think . . . it's . . . uh . . . a very sensual piece. I mean, the engine and the couple that interact with it are, well . . . you know . . . sexy." Speaker Gwen blushes.

"Okay," I roar, pounding the table with my fist. "She's on to me." The other women nod in agreement. The men shake their heads.

The delicate hairstylist at my right, a disciple of Garcia Marquez, begins a lengthy and convoluted discourse on word pictures. Dario knows just what to do with my piece to make it work but is unable to hold my attention. I look around the table, hoping someone will interpret.

"I don't know," says Burt. "I couldn't get past the first paragraph."

"I doubt any of us knows what a flywheel is," adds Chet, "and I've worked on a few car engines."

"You wouldn't just by chance be an engineer?" asks Burt.

"A *mechanical* engineer, perhaps?" chimes in Chet.

"With writing as an avocation?" teases Peg.

From my right, the belated but savvy Susan: "I think the relationship between the aging man and wife—they *are* older, aren't they? (I feel myself wizen)—is sweet and wonderful, such a welcome change from the bitterness shrouding most marriages today. And the woman, Witte. She's so competent. Why, she knows as much about the engine as her husband. I like a strong woman like that."

Wow, I think, furtively glancing at Gwen's huge eyes peering over the fruit tray. I've really done it: Validated my lesbian mother in print and cast a woman of substance. Tears well as I confirm that Witte is indeed a very special woman. And yes, I am her lucky husband Karcher, the engine doctor.

I've been watching Gwen put away strawberries like she'd had no supper. Her small, hypoglycemic face drains pale. She yawns and smiles sheepishly.

"I'm afraid I've had too much chocolate, and now I have a headache." The tray is empty. It's almost ten. I tell her I have a problem with sugar, too. She nods and forces another smile. I want to take her home. Alone. But she's married. And so am I.

Peg sets our next meeting for three weeks on a Wednesday. We make unsteady progress toward the door, heaping appreciation on

Toad for his hospitality. Dario goes home with Chet. The girls stick with me.

In the car, the conversation flits from shop talk to sex. The manuscript Gwen has dropped on us for next meeting's critique has a sex scene in it that Peg feels is too graphic. (Her heroine has a problem with the hydraulics.) Giggling from Gwen and Lori in the back seat. I watch their eyes in the mirror.

"You know, it's funny," Gwen reflects. "I'm attracted to unassuming men like Burt. They're such lovable teddy bears."

"Yeah, I know what you mean. We went out for coffee after class. He's nice," admits Lori.

"Sounds maternal," I jest, looking wistfully one last time at those huge eyes in the mirror. Witte has eyes like that, but they're iron gray. I shudder with pleasure at the thought. Witte is all mine.

Thermoil

To my great delight, Porter Lazier propped herself in a wheelchair under the north window of her Manhattan apartment, bent over the keys of her bible regal and began punctuating a Bach partita with impudent figures. She knew I loved her inventive interpretations which mimicked the precision grunts, clicks and knocks of my antique Thermoil one-cylinder engine. I sat facing her, alternately lifting the two weighted bellows as the diminutive organ's percussive brass reeds whined and growled between us. Now in our sixties, Porter and I had been making music together since 1980, shortly after she recovered from her accident.

* * * * * *

I met Porter at Tanglewood in 1977 under a sweltering August moon, my seventeen-year marriage to the good doctor D having ended amicably in July. I like to think the Davenports never accepted their eccentric son-in-law because his perpetually besmirched hands signaled a caste distinction, but the real motive for their rejection had to be disappointment at Joan's failure to rid me of a bipolar and paranoid proclivity.

I was on a well-deserved holiday from disapproval, touring the Dalton and Orange engine shows in Massachusetts with my Wurlitzer carousel organ. My friend Justin Pulsifer had asked to hear a new rag roll I'd arranged, to see if anyone could get around the incomplete Wurlitzer 150 scale without having to cheat. I was honored to accept the challenge from the famous ragtime scholar.

Arriving early on Saturday afternoon, I backed my creaky 1922 TT Ford truck off the trailer and centered it on the lawn in front of the music shell, making sure the organ faced the stage. As I made the rounds oiling the Thermoil, early arrivers gawked and asked the usual questions, but they were phrased in more erudite language.

"Young man (I was forty-seven), is that a steam calliope you intend on playing?" a dowager asked. "I do hope it won't interfere with our enjoyment of the concert."

"No, ma'am. Actually, it's a Style 146 Wurlitzer Military Band, a self-playing organ built in 1924 from a Coney Island carousel."

"What in heaven's name is a carousel organ doing at Tanglewood, and what is that thing on the back of it?"

"The Thermoil? That's an oil engine, ma'am. It cranks the organ." I bent on the flat leather belt linking the one-lunger to the organ's spiral-spoked wheel.

"Are you going to play it for us now?" asked her plump, goggle-eyed companion.

"I don't think Mr. Pulsifer would appreciate my interrupting his rehearsal." "America I Love You" could be heard leaking out of the barn a hundred yards to the north. "It'll be playing during intermission this evening. I hope you enjoy it."

One by one the curious circled the rig, pointed and whispered, shook their heads then meandered toward the refreshment stand. I decoupled the Thermoil's injector pushrod to ensure that it couldn't be started and joined the queue for iced tea. Those adjacent seemed offended by me and kept their distance, so I took my tea alone under the shade of a giant white oak and fell fast asleep.

It was nearly six when I was awakened by the repetitive chatter of a red squirrel practicing to be an auctioneer. Another skulk to the concession stand for a hamburger and I was ready to face the opposition on my own turf. Returning to the truck, I loaded the music roll and checked its tracking, closed the spool cabinet and waited in the cab for the concert to begin.

People began dotting the green with blankets topped with wicker baskets that dispensed wine and cheese. Goblets clinked and laughter sprang up all around. Everyone seemed stuffed with insincerity. My curious contraption stood like a grimy crane intruding on their pastoral party.

Justin put on a nostalgic program of one-steps, rags, cakewalks and marches. In no time his ensemble had them dancing around the truck, waving their glasses in time with the downbeats. They gave me sloppy smirks and gestured false approval at the 146 while intoxicating the close night air with off-pitch singing. My insecurity turned to disgust.

When the final strains of Sousa's "The Charlatan" died away, Justin announced my presence. "We have a special treat this evening. My friend Filson DeKleist has graciously agreed to play his antique Wurlitzer Military Band for our enjoyment during intermission. Now, I know some of you may take exception to the airing of mechanical music on these grounds. Please feel free to wander off if you find it offensive, although I'm afraid you'll have to vacate the premises to get out of earshot of these musicians. Seriously, I hope you'll tolerate this little diversion. I think the experience will enrich your music library."

With considerable trepidation, I relieved the compression, engaged the crank and spun it with all my might. Compression reinstated, several desultory blasts followed the first puff of white smoke out the stack. A minute later the Thermoil was up to speed, barking and panting like a St. Bernard. People crowded the rig. They were my audience now, wide eyed and sobering up.

Between the Thermoil's widely spaced reports you could hear the organ's wooden pump rods slapping their journals: "Ticka, tacka. Ticka, tacka. Ticka, tacka…" cranking the bellows and dragging the perforated paper down over the tracker bar. Abruptly as always, the holztrompette burst into double forte close harmony. The snare drum rasped from its perch atop a vestigial wing on the left side while the bass drum and cymbal crashed from a matching shelf on the right. From a rack on the façade, the octave violin screamed a simple obbligato. Deep inside the case the wood trombone groaned, the cello buzzed and the bourdon hooted.

Justin was delighted. When the last of the six selections, Joplin's "The Rag Time Dance," wound onto the spool, he clapped vigorously and gestured approval to the incredulous onlookers. The Wurlitzer exhausted a protracted sigh as it dumped vacuum for rewind. Relieved of the drag of the suction pump, the Thermoil huffed more than it barked. I scanned my audience of social climbers. From their expressions I deduced that the longhairs were indeed adding some notes to their musical vocabulary.

A slender woman in her early forties approached. She was wrapped in loose cotton chambray and bore the inquisitive scowl of a barred owl. Her large chestnut eyes searched my face for answers to questions I wasn't sure I wanted to hear. When she spoke, it was not the staccato, eight hoot sequence I was accustomed to hearing from such a visage, but the liquid, controlled coo of Grace Kelly.

"I've got to hand it to you. It takes guts to confront this group of intolerants with a music engine. I'm Porter Lazier from the *Times*." She extended a congruently narrow, velvety, manicured hand. "This must have been a harrowing experience for you." Smiling sympathetically, she added, "It's quite good. Better than I expected, actually." I feigned appreciation but my frown failed to convince my patchouli-scented opponent.

"I can see that my timing is bad. Maybe we can chat later, after the concert if you like?"

"Uh, sure. I guess so." I shut off the fuel and fiddled nervously with the oilers. There was something about her that prevented me from answering hostilely. I bedded down the Thermoil without looking up. When I turned around, she was gone.

I had the feeling I'd met someone transmitting on my frequency, yet there was no logical explanation for my reaction. Ms. Lazier wasn't especially attractive or charismatic; I'd never have approached her voluntarily. I felt intimidated by her dress and presentation, but my heart palpitated like that of a starving hypoglycemic.

I don't remember what Justin played or when the concert ended. I was slumped behind the wheel, staring without focus when Porter startled me by sliding into the cab and placing a small cassette recorder between us.

"Do you mind if I get some of this on tape?"

"Oh, uh. N… no. Be my guest," I became acutely aware of my filthy fingernails and sulfurous aroma. "You'll have to pardon my appearance. The Thermoil's a sloppy eater and refuses to be housebroken."

Ignoring my deprecation, Porter punched the record button and began the interview. "Tell me, Mr. DeKleist, what started you mixing music with machinery?"

I poured out my childhood, talked about falling asleep to the mournful melodies of César Franck and the minor minuets of Mozart's 40th and about the day I 'accidentally' broke those records, about the twelve-inch Victor 78 of Arthur Pryor playing Sousa's "El Capitan" with the pathos of a losing team's band that I marched to at Cub Scouts, about listening to the Gavioli organ at Savin Rock in West Haven, Connecticut, grind out four identical verses of the sinister J. Lawrence Cook arrangement of "The Spider And The Fly," about having to endure the pathetic moaning of my mother's 1939 Oldsmobile running out of battery on a damp morning, about reveling in the condensing steam and chuff of the Rollins Corliss at the L.C. Andrews sawmill in South Windham, Maine, about the terrifying roar of the diaphone fog horn at Two Lights, Cape Elizabeth, Maine, about the reliable thump of a Fairbanks-Morse Z sawing firewood, about the deafening blast of a Boston & Maine steam locomotive leaving Portland Union Station, and about being forced to practice the piano before supper.

I started to tell her about my alcoholic parents, the ostracism suffered by my gay brother and sister and their mutual suicide, but she stopped me.

"Filson. May I call you Filson? I'm not comfortable with this. Justin tells me you had problems arranging music for the Wurlitzer's forty-six note scale. I'd like to hear about that instead."

Porter's face brightened as I described the Wurlitzer's cryptic G, C, D bass with separately keyed reeds using up three more positions that should have been assigned to E, F and A, the missing sharps and the broken three and a half octave compass in four parts.

"Why, that's enough to give most arrangers nightmares. You worked a near miracle with that instrument. I would never have known its limitations from listening to your arrangements."

"You should hear some of the original fox-trots, waltzes and marches arranged by John William Tussing. Technically they're simplistic, full of repetition, incorrect notes and military phrasing, but, for me Tussing stumbled on the right formula. Under his imaginary baton, Wurlitzer organs sound at once mechanical and melancholy. Tussing's martial embellishments and tragic chords choke me up. He makes my 146 sound resolute and childlike as a doll piano.

"Regardless of the arranger though, one thing is certain: a Wurlitzer band organ is a sincere instrument. There's never a trace of frivolity in its voice. It works hard at making music, and it lets you know it. Sometimes it's painful listening to it struggling—all the earnest huffing and puffing, the relentless crashing of its traps, the simplistic oompah of its bass reeds, those missing sharps. But there's a message in its song, strength in its marching, endurance to work continuously for hours on end without rest and to carry on even when it's been neglected or mistreated. To some of us, it imparts those same qualities."

"Frankly, I think you've hit on the right formula. I want to hear more, but I'm afraid I must run. Got to get back to the city and write my review. Wasn't Justin wonderful?"

"I wish I could play all the instruments in his band at once."

"In a way, you have." She gestured toward the 146. "It was very nice meeting you, Filson. Here's my card. Look me up some time." Appearing to sense my disappointment, she added: "I really would like to hear more of your story when I'm not on deadline." Porter again extended her slender hand then slid away and vanished into the homebound throng as smoothly as she had arrived.

* * * * * *

I didn't hear from Porter again for almost two months. There was much to do fixing up the one room Vermont cabin I had acquired with the meager remains of my divorce settlement. Fortunately, the three-acre plot had a structurally sound barn and several chicken coops to shelter the Model TT Ford organ truck, the Fairbanks-Morse saw rig and my three other antique one-cylinder engines.

Walking out on Joan and the sea of white shirts at Sikorsky Aircraft were the best moves of my life. No more calculating stress concentrations, no more being forced to sign off on parts doomed to fail prematurely. No more sleepless nights. If the damn choppers crashed, it wasn't going to be my fault. I'd tried to beef up the main rotor shafts but my boss always overruled, citing monetary constraints or weight limits that were apparently more important than people's lives. It made me sick.

No more Joan nagging me to keep quiet and cooperate to avoid being fired. Why didn't *she* go out and work in the business world, get caught up in the hypocrisy of corporate ethics and lose some sleep alongside me? Oh, no. My self-appointed psychiatrist wife had to plot how to protect her primary patient (me) from himself, teach him to adjust to society, civilize him for the sake of our financial well-being.

Here in Vermont I had no one to answer to, be cajoled by, told how to dress, how to behave. I cut, split and delivered firewood between infrequent requests for music arrangements. It kept bread on the table and left me enough gas money to tour the engine shows on weekends. I slept well and felt full of vigor, but there was something missing.

* * * * * *

I was preparing to shut down the saw rig on a snappy early October afternoon when the Klaxon I'd wired to the telephone started honking from the porch. It was nearly five on a Thursday. A confident female voice on the other end said, "Oh, good, you're still alive. We have some unfinished business. You were going to tell me about your family and I got squeamish."

"Porter?"

"Surprised?"

"Yes. Listen, I've got a heap of hot iron banging away outside. Can I call you back?"

"Sure, as long as it's before ten. I have a proposition for you."

"Sounds ominous."

I hung up, dashed outside and closed the needle valve on the thrashing Fairbanks-Morse. Strangled, the old engine grunted impotently and began striking its magneto impulse coupling with a diminishing parade of clacks until its flywheels rolled to a stop and rocked back and forth several times. It was agonizing to witness the old girl struggle so to die, especially when the big circular saw rang out a dissonant death knell. Torn with emotion, I wiped the puddles from my eyes with a smudged shirtsleeve and headed for the cabin.

Back in the kitchen, I phoned Porter. "Sorry I had to cut you off." I snuffled into my armpit to clear my throat. "How are you?"

"I'm fine, but you sound all choked up. What happened?"

"Oh, that darned old Fairbanks one-lunger gets me every time I have to stop her. She tries so hard not to give up. It's pitiful."

"Listen, Filson, I need your help. I'd like you to come down and spend the weekend at Owl's Nest, my summer cottage on Bell Island off Branford, Connecticut. I go there in the off season to recharge. I figure you'd know how to revive the generator and my Evinrude outboard. Can you come?"

"Whoa, Porter. We hardly know each other. Are you sure you want a sentimental grease monkey loose in your linen?"

"I've sized you up as the trustworthy type, one that wouldn't think of taking advantage of a helpless, single newspaperwoman."

"You're right. I've had enough woman trouble to last me a lifetime."

"It's a date then. I'll be at the Stony Creek dock at four tomorrow afternoon."

Ignoring my feeble protest, Porter rattled off directions and excused herself to a background pecking of keyboards.

I put the phone gently back on its cradle and sank into my bentwood cedar rocker, letting the warm memory of Porter's inquisitive face float in the heat waves rising from the Jotul wood stove as I watched the sun's orange ball sink behind the pines. A wisp of steam rising from the saw rig outside reminded me to drain the engine's water hopper before it froze. A chicken watering pot went over the stack, a worn out bicycle tire wrapped the saw blade and an olive drab tarp covered the rig. I patted the warm canvas. "Good old girl. I can always depend on you."

After supper I tried to finish a fox-trot arrangement of "Chiribiribin" for the Wurlitzer 165 scale but couldn't concentrate, so I threw some clothes in a duffel and reloaded the stove.

Tired as I was, apprehension saw to it that I slept fitfully. The half-moon appeared consecutively framed in each of the six panes of my window as I paced the room. The saw rig, silhouetted against the moonlit sky, resembled a sperm whale floating on a sea of frost. Far to the east a Great Horned owl hooted the hour of five. At six the neighbor's roosters awoke, and I gave up trying to sleep.

* * * * * *

My organ tow truck, a work worn '68 F250 4x4 pickup, was hardly suitable expressway transportation. It rode like an ATV and wandered at will, requiring constant steering corrections just to stay within the lane, but it got me to Connecticut. I rumbled to a stop on the Stony Creek quay at ten of four, exhausted and red-eyed after five hours of sawing the wheel.

Porter was standing at the top of the ramp, leaning against the handrail, watching the gulls swoop and wheel over the harbor. Her oversize hooded sweater nearly reached her knees, leaving just a foot of blue denim showing above her mukluks. Hearing the Ford crunch to a halt in the crushed clam shells, she turned and beamed broadly.

As I swung my duffel out of the pickup bed, she reached my side, looking radiantly rosy and puffing question marks into the cool air. "You look ready for a mug of tea by the fire. How long did it take you?"

"About five hours. I don't usually drive this far for an engine, much less a woman. How far is the island?"

"A mile or so. Can you row?"

"Don't you have a motor?"

"That's what I was trying to tell you on the phone. The outboard ingested some salt water last weekend and refuses to start. Come on; the exercise will do you good."

"Thanks—I think."

We stepped aboard a shapely Whitehall rowboat badly in need of paint. Porter took to the stern sheets while I settled myself at the forward thwart to pull us out to sea. The slender spruce spoon oars were nicely balanced and we made good way in the ebbing tide. Porter kept me on course with her dainty, mittened hand.

"Stay outside nun 12," she warned as we approached a leaning red cone that trailed a wake in our direction. "You've pulled a few oars in your time. Who taught you to row like that?"

"My mother. She was quite the seaman."

"Sea person."

"No, in her case, sea *man*. She was bisexual and wore the pants in the family. Discipline and manual training were freely given. Hugging and kissing were for sissies."

"I see. And what about your father?"

"He was an old softy. Loved classical music and books, pink sunsets and the rose Peace. Sweet man, but devastated. I pitied him being married to her."

We slid onto a bed of kelp at low tide. The dock was a slippery twenty paces inshore, no problem in the right footwear, but I had on smooth-soled work boots. Down I went on my butt as soon as I stepped into the ooze. Porter giggled, brushed me off and braced my arm as we negotiated the treacherous slime.

"You remind me of a seal. Graceful as a fish in water but clumsy as an ox on land."

"Ouch."

"Sorry. That was flip of me. Let's get something hot into you."

Porter ushered me into a sparsely furnished, musty little cottage with linoleum floors and kerosene lamps. It had a primitive electric service that had obviously not been in use for several years, judging from the cobwebbed and empty fuse panel and the barren electric sconces.

"How did they get power to the island?"

A small voice from the kitchen said, "That's the other thing I hoped you might look into. The generator out on the rock died the summer before last."

Normally I would have been flattered to be asked to mechanically assist a damsel in distress, but this was getting to feel like pressure. A part of me wanted to get involved—much more involved—but I kept stepping on that part, hoping it would go away. "I'm afraid I didn't bring any tools."

"There are some in the powerhouse."

Porter rustled up some kindling and started a fire in the potbelly while I slouched on the couch and tried to make sense of my prescribed mission. A few minutes later, Porter placed a steaming pot of Lapsang Souchong in front of me. Her jaw muscles had tightened and her speech was clipped. "Have some tea, Filson, before you get greasy."

There was urgency in her manner that I couldn't fathom at the time. Was she afraid I might take advantage of her and therefore anxious to get my hands dirty working on the generator? Or was she afraid I'd think she was flirting if she didn't keep the subject of tired iron on the table?

"I'll look at the generator tomorrow, okay?"

I took a sip of tea and sighed. "Being married to a manipulative woman for seventeen years and, having extricated myself, I vowed to control the balance of my life."

Porter's lips firmed and lost their color. She returned to the kitchen and began opening Dinty Moore cans for supper, trying to break the vacuum seals as unobtrusively as possible. We consumed the stew in silence under the glare of an Aladdin lamp. I finished first.

"I'm sorry I snapped at you like that. Autonomy becomes a consuming goal after being led by the nose by domineering if well-meaning women, starting with my mother. I hope you're not another one."

Porter's eyes puddled. "The truth is, I haven't the money to keep this place in repair. Owl's Nest was my family's summer home. I inherited it five years ago." She paused to snuff back her tears. "Look, I'm stuck, Filson. Remembering how you liked engines and that sort of thing, I really thought you might enjoy helping me with the outboard and the generator. I don't think they need much."

"You certainly are persistent. I envisioned a lost weekend on a deserted island with an attractive woman. You know—snuggling by the fire while the wind howls in the screens."

"Filson, I'm scared. It's been almost three years since Frank died. We were married for twelve years. He was a novelist. Sensitive, sweet man." A sigh interrupted her narrative. "Poor guy. He didn't know a spark plug from a household fuse."

"He sounds like my father. Speaking of fuses, where are they?"

"In the kitchen drawer."

"Good. Another night's sleep won't hurt 'em. Tomorrow's soon enough to disturb the cobwebs. Let's talk about us."

"I thought we were."

"You're a tough lady. Guess you've gotta be tough to survive the Big Apple. Me? I go for the nurturing type: soft, soothing and devoted."

Porter's face turned crimson. "You bastard! How dare you even think you've got me trapped?" She slammed her fist down on the table, making the teapot rattle. "Consider this, fella: there's only one way off Bell Island this time of year." She paused. "Yup, the way we came. And if I get to the boat first, you'll be marooned." She grabbed her parka and bolted from the cabin.

By the time I got to my feet and gave chase, she was half way to the boat on a dead run. It was forty-five degrees and dark. I tripped on a rock, skidded on some kelp and crashed into a beach plum. By the time I freed myself from the thorns, she had taken command of our vessel and was pulling away from shore and calling from the helm, "Perhaps your mommy will rescue you from the Wicked Witch of the West."

I was dumbfounded. There I stood, without a coat, perched on a deserted island, watching my only way ashore go out to sea.

Porter disappeared into the mist heading northwest toward the mainland. I called after her several times but she didn't reply. Nothing to do but let her cool off; that, I figured, wouldn't take long on such a night. I picked my way back to the cottage and waited.

A Regulator pendulum clock over the sofa struck nine. That intrigued me because I didn't remember Porter winding it. I checked the Myers pump at the kitchen sink. It was primed; of course it was, Porter had made tea. But I didn't see her prime it. Neither the clock nor the pump would have been working after a week or more's absence. A chill ran the length of my spine. "What the hell is going on here?"

Porter had described herself as Bell Island's only inhabitant. Well, not in so many words, but that was the inference I gathered from her brief account. The more I thought about it, the less sure I was about just what she had said. I began to tremble like a little kid in the haunted house at Old Orchard Beach.

I tried not to breathe and lowered myself slowly into a stuffed chair by the window, listening with maximum acuity. A half hour passed without incident. All I heard was the wind sighing and the leaves rustling about the cottage.

My thoughts drifted back to Porter. Why did she take off like that? She seemed prone to sudden, wide mood swings hair-triggered by ordinary circumstances. Like my mother used to say about me, Porter could be volatile as winter gasoline.

About 9:40 I became aware of a moving pinpoint of light outside the window. It seemed to be advancing from the general direction of the dock. My heart quickened. Good, I thought, Porter's returned.

A moment later I heard a knock at the door, the gentle knock of someone trying not to interrupt. I hesitated before rising to answer. Porter would have walked right in; the door wasn't even locked.

Cracking the door cautiously, I peeked into the blackness. A wizened old woman was on the doorstep, flashlight in hand. She began in a scratchy whine: "Is everything all right, dear? I saw the boat leaving. Was there someone with you?"

I realized she hadn't seen me, and neither had she noticed who was in the boat. Opening the door and revealing my identity gave her quite a start.

"Oh, gracious me, I thought you were Porter. Where is she?"

"Out in the boat. I'm a friend, Filson DeKleist. Who are you?"

"They call me Hattie. I watch over things while she's away. She's an odd girl. Mostly alone. Doesn't bring visitors very often." Hattie shook her head. "I worked for Porter's folks till they passed away. Porter asked me to stay on, but I can't do much anymore." She frowned. "What's she doing out in the boat on a night like this?"

"We had a disagreement. She'll be back soon, I'm sure. Won't you come in?"

"No thanks. I just wanted to see if everything was to her liking. I'm over on the west side of the island if you need anything." Hattie trudged off down the path, waving as she turned the corner.

The Wicked Witch of the West. Very funny. Well, that explains the wound clock and the primed pump. Feeling childish for getting so worked up, I fed the stove a few splits of birch and curled up on the couch with a tattered copy of *A Hat-Tub Tale* by Caroline Dwight Emerson, the comforting story of Tuck, a kindly vegetarian bear who makes salads with his spoon paw and fork paw in a tiny cottage high above the Bay of Fundy, who rescues Nip, a testy water rat equipped with a fish hook at the end of his tail, tempers his irascible friend in a hat-tub bath in front of the fire and invites him to stay. Tuck was just admonishing Nip for storing his smelly fish under the bed, when I fell asleep.

I awoke at six-thirty to the moaning of the Penfield Reef horn. During the night fog had rolled in, casting the cottage in a ghostly glow. Feeling as guilty as Nip, I picked my way down to the dock and squinted in the whiteness. The boat was still gone. The sea was calm. I strained to hear sounds of life between the horn's mournful cries.

Better notify Hattie. Let's see, west is over there, I think. It was difficult to get a bearing in the fog, but I found a path that appeared to follow the shoreline and turned left to follow it. The path broke into the open several times where it crossed granite outcrops; one was so vast that I lost my direction and apparently headed inland. Out of the fog, near the top of the gently rising rock, a small, weathered shed appeared. This couldn't be Hattie's place.

I quickened my pace. As I approached the shed I could see wires emanating from a porcelain fixture under the roof. This must be the powerhouse that Porter had referred to. I forgot my mission and began exploring.

Back of the shed stood a rusty oval fuel tank. I rapped on it and determined that it was about half full. A black exhaust pipe poked out one side with its exit facing downward to exclude the elements. The door was padlocked but the hasp was so rusted, I was able to pry it free with a stake of rebar I found lying under the tank. The Z-braced door swung open and I stepped up on the sill.

The familiar odor of kerosene, hard grease and cold iron told me I'd found the right place. As I stood in the doorway waiting for my eyes to adjust to the dim light, a dark mass centered in the shadows began to take shape until I could recognize the distinctive lines of a Fairbanks-Morse ZC lighting plant dating from the forties. My pulse quickened, and I felt drawn inside, but a flash of anger stopped me from entering. With Porter abandoning me like that, why should I fix her damn generator? There wasn't sufficient natural light to do any work, anyway.

Then I noticed the Raytheon radiotelephone hanging on the front wall next to the door, apparently Bell Island's only means of communication. Without power, it was useless. If I could get the generator started, I might be able to call for help.

With clenched teeth, I went inside. A kerosene lantern stood on a workbench in the corner. I found a match and lit the wick. Fingers crossed, lamp in hand, I approached the generator to assess its condition. The valves were free so I tugged at one of the engine's twin flywheels. Getting no response, I stood on a spoke. Nothing. My heart sank. In desperation I jumped on the spoke with both feet. I heard a click and the spoke slowly lowered, depositing me gently on the floor.

After rocking the engine several times to limber it up, checking its magneto for spark, cleaning the plug and satisfying myself that there was sufficient oil in the base and coolant in the radiator, I put a pan under the fuel strainer petcock and drew off almost a quart of water before I got to the fuel. The gasoline smelled rancid, but it was worth a try.

I choked the Fairbanks and bled off some compression so I could turn it past top dead center. One heave on the flywheels was all it took to make the beast blat a tongue of flame from its stack. Four heavy cannon reports later the plant was up to speed, steadily gulping and thudding, blowing smoke rings into the fog. I watched the naked light bulb dangling from its cord overhead come to life. At first a dull orange glow, its color lightened through lemon to cream as the voltage stabilized.

Pride of accomplishment was quickly extinguished by the nagging realization that Porter's extended absence could mean only one of two things: She'd gone ashore and perhaps driven back to Manhattan in a huff, or she never made land and was floundering about in the fog, lost and perhaps in danger. I reached for the Raytheon's receiver. It was difficult to hear over all the whumping and flapping, but I managed to get a call out to the Coast Guard. After three tries I heard a young male voice in a southern accent reply. "Roger, Bell Island. How may we be of service? Over."

I had just finished describing my predicament when Hattie appeared in the doorway, wringing her hands and grinning like a jack-o-lantern. I nodded an acknowledgement to her while requesting the officer on the radio to check the quay at Stony Creek for Porter's Subaru. If it was gone, I could at least breathe a little easier. If not, the men in blue had their work cut out for them. Even with radar, finding a rowboat in such a fog would be like looking for a four leaf clover with a flashlight. Before signing off I agreed to remake contact at noon. It was then about nine.

Hattie bubbled with excitement. "We haven't had electricity for nearly two years. I was fixing some eggs on the wood range when all of a sudden the kitchen light came on, the refrigerator began humming and the mantle clock began to wind itself. Scared me half to death." She peered into the shed. "How'd you fix it?"

"Water in the gas, mainly, from condensation in the tank. The engine was stuck, but it came free when I jumped on it. Spark plug was a little dirty. No big one."

"Oh, I'm so glad. Porter will be really pleased. She always had a terrible time starting it." She paused and her brow furrowed. "Where *is* Porter? And who was that you had on the phone?" She hadn't heard my conversation from the doorway over the din of the generator.

I guided Hattie outside where we could hear one another. "I don't want to alarm you, but Porter's still AWOL. She never came back last night. I've asked the Coast Guard to assist. First they're going to check to see if her car is still parked at Stony Creek."

"Oh, Lord, no! Poor thing. She always was headstrong. Feisty wisp of a girl. Thought she could do everything herself. Never wanted any help. I warned her that being stubborn would one day kick back." Hattie's mouth turned down at the corners. I put my arm around her shoulder. She tried to smile but a tear trickled down one cheek and she had to look away. After a brief silence she seemed to brighten up. "I have an idea. My dory's still serviceable. When the fog lifts we can row you ashore. I'm willing to bet she's back in the city sulking. She knew I'd find you. It's just like her to pull a tantrum."

"I think we should wait for the Coast Guard to complete their preliminary investigation. Besides, this fog's going to be around awhile. The water's warmer than the air."

We closed and braced the door on the shed. Hattie led the way as we descended the outcrop. Reluctant to leave, I looked back over my shoulder at the parade of puffs leaving the exhaust pipe as the generator pounded away inside its little house. The tear in my eye was not for Porter. In the cruel world of perpetual human failure, the faithful one-lunger sounded a poignant note of security to one who keenly felt life's irony.

* * * * * *

Hattie's cabin was as cozy as Porter's was chilling: natural cedar walls, the aroma of baking bread from a cast iron Atlantic range chortling contentedly on its diet of oak, and braided rugs on the wide pine floor boards with a needle point welcome sign over the refrigerator that proclaimed, 'Have another helping on Hattie.' I did, and a good thing, too, for it would be my last meal for the next twenty-four hours. Fortified with freshly baked stollen, bacon and eggs she kept in the ice chest on the porch and black coffee, back up the hill we went to call the Coast Guard.

The faithful Fairbanks had succeeded in warming the shed to a comfortable sixty-eight degrees in our absence. A pall of partially oxidized hydrocarbons blown past the piston rings greeted our nostrils. I fanned the door and propped open the sash nearest the radio. "Poor thing's trying to asphyxiate itself." I made strangling gestures as I exited.

Hattie, standing outside, was in no mood for levity. "Better get on the air. You'll need all the daylight you can muster to…" Her voice choked to a halt. She snuffed back tears and tried again. "They may need you to…God punish me for what I'm thinking."

I hesitated before reentering the smoky shed. It wasn't the atmosphere, which I rather liked, unwholesome as it was, but fear of hearing the worst that troubled me. Hattie pointed to the hour of midday on her watch and I reached for the radio. Through the crackling hiss came the familiar southern drawl, "Bell Island, this is cutter seventy-nine. Over."

"Did you find the car, sir? Over."

"Affirmative. Red 1978 Subaru sedan, New York plates PL 157, facing south on Stony Creek quay. Sea search in progress, nun twelve south to Gull Rock, northeast to Dawson's Island, north to Cormorant Ledge. Search area visibility twenty-five feet. Over."

I shuddered. "Is there anything we can do here to help? Over."

Again, the chilling monotone, "Negative. Can you maintain power? Over."

"Yes, I think so. We have fuel for about another eighteen hours. Over."

"Good. Monitor channel 23. We may need identification. Out."

I switched channels, turned on the loudspeaker and adjusted the gain, but all we could hear over the generator was a lifeless hiss. I looked at Hattie. She was sitting on the granite doorstep with her head in her hands. I wanted to reach out and comfort her but I was too angry at myself for triggering Porter's tantrum.

I crouched next to Hattie, steeped in sorrow, and only became aware of my surroundings again when she tapped me on the shoulder. "Filson, are you all right?"

"They've got to find her. I couldn't live with the guilt if the sea takes her."

"Don't be so hard on yourself. They'll find her. Say, I think the fog is lifting a little."

"I'm going out there. It's the least I can do. May I use your dory?"

"Don't be a fool, Filson. They're professionals and they have radar. You don't even have a motor."

"Hattie, can you stay here and listen for bulletins? I'll be back in two hours. The generator should be all right."

Hattie shook her head and muttered something unintelligible as I made the rounds, checking the generator's vital signs. At the door I broke into a run. The path was just visible in the mist, and I arrived at Hattie's cabin on the shore in less than five minutes. The dory was aground, lashed to a piling in the reeds. There was no time to wait for the tide. I wrestled the sodden hulk across the mud to the water's edge and shoved off. Never having rowed with thole pins before, I was thankful there was no audience. After unshipping the oars several times, I learned to pitch them so they pressed down on the gunwales when I pulled. I got the dory moving pretty well and began to relax to the rhythmic thump of the looms against the pins.

The fog had abated sufficiently that I could see several hundred feet of shoreline. I reasoned that Porter had intended to row for Stony Creek but had gotten turned around in the fog and headed toward Long Island. Sticking close to the Bell Island shore, I set a seaward course. By the time I reached the southern tip of the island, the visibility had improved to half a mile.

When Penfield Reef stopped moaning I knew I had a chance at finding Porter. Keeping the island in sight for a bearing, I continued south, glancing over my shoulder every once in a while. Nothing but gentle swells ahead.

Far astern I could now just make out the Coast Guard cutter plying the Connecticut coast as I had figured. Dummies, I thought. They don't know Porter. Upon reflection, neither did I.

The strengthening sun felt good on my tired back muscles. It was going to be an Indian summer afternoon with temperatures in the sixties and a balmy southwesterly breeze. The water's surface rippled and darkened as the air began to move. I was just getting in tune with nature when I noticed a speck on the surface almost dead ahead. My pulse quickened. Probably just a gull looking deceptively distant, I tried telling myself, but my body knew better and began supplying the adrenalin I needed to close the gap.

Twenty minutes later I knew it was not a gull. It was the Whitehall, or what remained of it. The bow was gone and the hind quarters jutted just above the surface. Both oars had long since drifted out of sight. Porter's head was lying on the stern seat, her face nearly awash with each swell that came aboard. The rest of her was jammed under the center thwart. She was a ghastly blue, unconscious and apparently in shock.

I don't remember pulling the last fifty yards or how I got her aboard the dory. Things began to happen fast. The throb of the 79's Cummins diesels close off the starboard bow startled me. A loudspeaker crackled from the cutter's bridge. "We'll take it from here. Heave to and ship your oars. We're coming alongside."

I looked over my shoulder to see the cutter towering over us, deploying a sling from its gin pole. Men in blue were scurrying about the deck securing lines, tailing the winch and setting out a stretcher. Ropes went over the side and two young cadets slithered down to secure the sling around the dory. Moments later, we were hoisted aboard and deposited gently on the deck. An officer heavily encrusted with medals and badges approached. "Are you Filson DeKleist?" I nodded an affirmative. "Looks like you reached her just in time."

An efficient CPR team surrounded Porter. She was rolled onto her stomach, emptied of salt water, bundled in blankets and carefully lifted onto the stretcher while the 79 made full knots for New Haven harbor. I watched Porter slip in and out of consciousness, never able to speak. We arrived at the Coast Guard station in less than twenty minutes, but it seemed like an hour. The ambulance was waiting.

A new team of medics took over, an IV was started, and we were whisked to Yale-New Haven Hospital accompanied by the sterile, programmed whoop of the electronic siren. Porter was transferred to a gurney and unceremoniously rolled into the bowels of the hospital, leaving me gaping at a pair of swinging doors whose motion gradually damped to a standstill.

A soothing female voice behind me said, "We'd like to get some background information on Ms. Lazier. Please have a seat." I turned to see a comely young police detective smiling up at me and gesturing to a chair. I introduced myself and related my theory as to how the accident happened, omitting the details of what prompted Porter to venture out on the sound.

Almost immediately, I regretted being vague and ambiguous. She obviously wasn't buying my story. Still smiling sweetly, she began interrogating me as if I'd committed a crime. "What took place just prior to Ms. Lazier's departure?"

If I come clean now, I thought, she'll suspect me guilty of skullduggery and assume the worst. My mind conjured the criminal possibilities: I flew into a rage and beat Porter unconscious because she refused me and was in the process of transporting her body to a watery grave far from land when the Coast Guard caught me in the act and accepted my hastily contrived story of her rescue from the sinking Whitehall. I used the radiotelephone to set up the Coast Guard for a lengthy and futile search for Porter's shipwreck near the mainland, then rowed her unconscious body out to sea, intending to dispose of it and return to Bell Island to convince Hattie that my search was in vain, but the cutter sneaked up on me, and again the authorities believe my valiant recount of Porter's rescue.

Judging from the angle of the detective's head and her raised eyebrows, I deduced that I had to be more convincing. "Porter and I grew up together. Although we followed different tracks over the years, we've remained the best of friends. It was only natural that Hattie, Porter's caretaker, phone me when she didn't show up on Friday. I got down here as quickly as I could. Hattie met me at the dock with her dory. After depositing her on the island with instructions to monitor the rescue channel, I set out to try and find Porter myself. The rest you know."

Full of holes as the story was, I figured the police wouldn't bother to check the details. How wrong I was.

The detective politely pretended to accept my tale, nodding and um-humming appropriately at intervals while scratching notes on a pad. When I finished, she rose and took her leave, closing with, "Thank you for your cooperation, Mr. DeKleist. Please remain in town in case we have further questions."

Freed from the hot seat, I inquired at the desk as to Porter's condition and was told that she was still being examined in the ER. I was invited to wait in the lobby and help myself to coffee; it might be some time, the receptionist said, before the doctor could report her condition. I took a seat in the waiting room, grabbed the latest *New Yorker* and tried to fathom the meaning of a poem on page ten.

The longer I sat there, the more uneasy I felt. I was getting nowhere with the poem. And instead of feeling concern for Porter, I was mulling over my contrived crime. It was nearly midnight when a tall, freshly trained neurologist approached with a troubled expression. I squirmed in my chair before rising to greet him. "I'm Filson DeKleist, a friend of Porter's. How is she?"

The doctor's frown deepened. "I'm afraid Ms. Lazier received a heavy blow at the base of her skull. She's paralyzed from the waist down. We won't know for several days how permanent the disability is, but I'm not optimistic about her full recovery. Fewer than twenty percent of patients in her condition ever walk again." He paused to allow the gravity of his message to sink in. "You were not with her when it happened, I understand."

"No, I was ashore. Listen, is she conscious? Can I see her?"

"She's been heavily sedated, and I'm afraid I cannot allow you to visit until the police have concluded their examination."

"The police? I've just told them what happened. Why do they need to question her? Hasn't she been through enough?"

"Routine. Whenever there's an incident like this, they run an investigation, just to be sure there hasn't been any foul play. You know how the law works."

"Yeah. They close in on the hapless victim before she's even had a chance to get medical attention, eager to squeeze a juicy story—if they're lucky, a gruesome tale of aborted murder—from their half-conscious patient just before she dies. Thoughtless bastards!"

The young doctor seemed mildly amused. "Ms. Lazier isn't critical, Mr. DeKleist. She'll be able to receive family and friends once the police establish a corroborated story that satisfies their curiosity. Now, why don't you try and get some rest." He smiled condescendingly, turned and merged with his antiseptic white surroundings.

* * * * * *

It was nearly one when I reached the street. I stood a moment outside the hospital lobby, reviewing the odds like a criminal out on bail. What if Porter had been sufficiently coherent to tell the police the truth? Worse, what if she was demented as a result of her injury or so angry that she had blurted out a saga of attempted rape, abuse and abandonment? Hattie was my only hope. She could confirm my story. But I'd told a fib to the police. I had to get to her before they did and make sure she told them the same lie. But how? The Coast Guard had her dory and I had no way to get to the island. The Coast Guard. That's it. They knew the truth. They'd clear up the whole issue.

Wait a minute. The Coast Guard knew only what I told them on the radio and what they saw at sea. I could easily have done Porter in for all they knew. But they hadn't disputed my story. They might help me again.

Pulling my collar up around my neck in an attempt to disguise my profile, I headed for the nearest pay phone and called my maritime friends. They had no trouble identifying me.

"Oh, yes, Mr. DeKleist. The police have filled us in on the details of their investigation. They seem to be looking for a motive." The cadet paused. "How is Ms. Lazier?"

I relayed her condition and my plight. My heart sank as I heard what had happened since we were deposited at the hospital. The police had impounded Hattie's dory, they said, and they were very sorry, but they couldn't help me further.

"Could you at least get a message to Porter's caretaker on the island? She'll be worried sick."

"The mail boat will be stopping there tomorrow. They can take your message, sir. We wish Ms. Lazier a speedy recovery."

Of course, the mail boat. I could hitch a ride out on the morning run, prime Hattie and return in time to see Porter before visiting hours ended. I walked to Union Station, grabbed a taxi and got a room at the 76 Truck Stop which was only a couple miles from the dock. After spending a dreadful night chastising myself for lying to the police, I hoofed it to Stony Creek, paid my fare and settled on the engine box of the old fish boat that ran the island circuit. There were no other passengers.

"Never seen you aboard my boat. I'm Roy Capper. Folks call me Cap." The crusty lobsterman flashed me a wry smile and got us underway. Raising his voice and calling over his shoulder, he said, "Woman over on Bell Island nearly got bumped off out here night before last. Coast Guard found her out near Gull Rock. There was a man in the boat with her. She'd been struck unconscious back of the neck. They think he's the one that done it. Gruesome." He paused. "Where you headed? You didn't say."

It was no use. I was trapped and had to come clean. In the remaining minutes before we docked at Bell Island, I blurted out the true story, all of it, but Cap wasn't buying. The more I related, the larger grew his derisive grin. He didn't refute my story and he didn't threaten me, but it was crystal clear from his expression that he'd hooked a big fish and intended on playing it until he could reel it in.

As we approached the dock I could see Hattie pacing anxiously on the float. She was surprised and very pleased to see me, and pumped me full of questions before I could drag her out of earshot of my maritime jailer. I brought her up to date while Cap offloaded her provisions into a rusty cart. We were all on the float when panic struck me.

I got to the part where the detective approached me in the hospital and broke off mid-sentence. Hattie, who had been hanging on my every word, looked up at me with a bulldog expression of concern. Cap, anxious to get underway, gestured for me to climb aboard. Something inside me snapped and I dashed up the ramp, along the dock and into the brambles in the direction of the powerhouse. At the first clearing I stopped to look back. The path was deserted and I could hear the mail boat burbling away from the float. Feeling much relieved, I walked the rest of the way to the powerhouse. I hated to run from Hattie, but I had to be sure we were alone on the island.

The generator had run out of fuel and grown cold. The spare gas cans were empty. With the radio dead, I was now truly marooned with no way to contact the mainland. The mail boat wouldn't be back for a week. Thank God for Hattie. At least I could get a square meal.

Cap's boat was no longer visible, but I could still hear the rumble of its engine gradually diminishing in the distance. When I could no longer hear it, I felt it safe to strike out for Hattie's place.

I found Hattie sitting on her doorstep holding onto her cart full of provisions. She kept shaking her head and repeating, "Oh, my. Oh, my." I sat down beside her and waited. After a few minutes she seemed to have settled down sufficiently to absorb my complicated predicament.

"Cap will be back, you know." She looked hard at me. "He knows you can't get off the island now. He'll be glued to the TV, waiting for the police to announce the man hunt and perhaps offer a reward for information leading to your arrest. When the stakes get high enough, he'll come forward and offer you up for ransom."

"Hattie, do you have a portable radio?"

"Top of the kitchen counter."

"Good, we can keep abreast of the search, if there is to be one, and be able to gauge when they might come back for me. Better yet, you monitor the radio. I've got work to do, and there isn't much time. Do you have an axe?"

"Sure. In the woodshed. Why?"

"When I was a Scout, we learned how to make a logomaran, a crude outrigger canoe made out of logs and saplings. It was intended for crossing shallow streams. You stood on the big center log 'hull' which was stabilized by a pair of small log floats bridged to either side by the saplings, and poled the thing along. Of course, out here on the Sound, I'd need a long oar or paddle."

"Filson, have you gone mad? Do you want to wind up like Porter, all busted up in the hospital?"

"No, really. The thing could get me to shore, at night when it's calm. I'm going scouting for suitable wood." I fetched the axe, touched up its edge with a stone Hattie kept on the shelf, and headed outside.

I found just what I was looking for not five hundred yards down the path: a gnarled, venerable red cedar, dead dry but still standing. The butt was large enough for the hull, and I figured the upper trunk would do fine for the floats. I had the stark, silvery cedar down, limbed and cut to length inside an hour. Two green ash saplings nearby were sacrificed for the outriggers. After cutting the notches, I lashed the five pieces together with clothesline. After hewing a couple of footholds in the side of the main log I went in search of a plank for the paddle.

Fortunately, there was still some spruce staging stored under Hattie's porch. I found a board about six feet long and fashioned a crude paddle with my jackknife. By sundown I was ready. After Hattie had once again fortified me with a hearty meal, I dragged the logomaran down to the shore and tested its buoyancy. To my surprise, the raft kept me above the surface, barely, and I pushed off toward Stony Creek on the remains of the afternoon swell. Hattie was standing on the porch, still shaking her head.

The bracing night urged me to pull hard to keep warm. I soon got into a pattern of paddling two quick strokes to port then switching to starboard for two strokes and back again to port, to keep the thing going mostly straight. With a canopy of stars above and the shore lights ahead growing gradually larger, I kept my courage through several near capsizes as the logomaran rolled precariously between swells under my shifting weight, submerging first one float then the other as the wood became waterlogged and began losing buoyancy.

After what seemed like an hour I reached the pier. By then I was ankle deep in the fifty degree Long Island Sound and had lost all feeling in my feet. Flopping down on the deserted float, I cut the cords binding the logomaran together, set the three chunks of cedar adrift and flung the two saplings out to sea with all the strength I could muster. Now devoid of my craft, from all appearances I had walked on water.

Once I'd worked some circulation back into my numb toes so I could walk, I headed for my truck. Porter's Subaru was still parked on the other side of the lot. I sat for several minutes in the truck, contemplating my alternatives. Only two came to mind. Common sense told me to make straight for home, lie low, and hope the authorities wouldn't extradite. But my heart was tugging me to the hospital where I would have to give myself up for one last glimpse of Porter. Although the radio had mentioned nothing of the incident, I couldn't suppress the eerie feeling that I was being hunted.

It was more guilt than concern that drew me back to Porter. If I hurried, I could just get in before the close of visiting hours. After a dozen furtive glances in the mirror I began to relax.

The hospital was in its usual state of mild panic, but there were no police in sight. The receptionist said that Porter was fully conscious and able to receive visitors. No mention of the investigation or the previous police shutout. I entered Porter's room feeling much relieved.

Porter was seated on her bed, staring, motionless out the window. Her disheveled hair was caked with the salt of a day's grief expressed. She did not turn to face me or otherwise acknowledge my presence for a minute or two. "Porter, I…I got here as quick as I could. Hattie knows. She's…we're so worried. How are you?"

Slowly, her wan, tear-stained face turned in my direction. Gone was the spark of curiosity in her huge brown eyes. Instead, I saw the glassy stare of a stuffed barred owl cut down by a hunter's bullet. I could neither advance nor retreat from the fifth tile from the door that I stood on.

"Filson, I didn't expect to ever see you again."

I moved toward her but the narrowing of her eyes, which now took dead aim for mine, stopped me before I reached the bed. Her mouth opened again to speak, drawing a pasty string of saliva between her lips that tore away with her next words. "Woman trouble? You said you'd had your fill. Apparently not."

The color returned to her cheeks and she began to shake. "Worried? I'll bet you're worried. You missed an inquisition. It was better than on TV. Funny, they believed me. I told them the truth. Wish you had."

I approached the bed and reached out for her hand, but she recoiled. "Gee, you don't look much like a fugitive to me. But then, I hardly know you." A trace of a smile flickered across her face. "Stupid cops. They were convinced you were some kind of a pervert on a rampage." She exhausted a protracted sigh. "There isn't going to be an investigation. It's over. I convinced them it was an accident. The tanker never saw me in the fog and almost cut the Whitehall in half. I'm lucky to be alive."

"You mean I've been running away from nothing."

She rolled her eyes. "I missed my opportunity. I should have made up a juicy tale of attempted rape and aborted murder at sea."

"Porter, I'm so sorry. I...."

"No, you're not. Your engines mean more to you than I do. Let's just call a truce and go our separate ways."

"I was hoping we could put aside our differences and be friends. We have at least two things in common, volatile personalities and the love of music.

"My role models, my alcoholic parents, were so unstable, I mistrusted everyone and kept as far away from people as possible. The engines became my friends because they were dependable and predictable. When I was a child, I believed that humans would be wiped off the earth and the steadfast one-cylinder engines would take over. I wanted to be the one fleshy thing left to witness that transformation. As a teen arriving home after a school social, when my father asked me how I enjoyed dancing, I said, 'I went to the dance thinking about one-cylinder engines and I left the dance thinking about one cylinder engines.' I didn't dare think about girls."

Porter looked down at her legs. "I'm not much good to anyone now. You see, I...the doctor said there's nothing he can do. I'm...." Porter choked to a stop and averted her gaze to hide her tears.

"Don't, Porter. I know." I slid beside her and buried my face in her fragrant neck. This time there was no protest. Her slender arms encircled my head as she sobbed.

"I, too, had a bizarre childhood. My mother committed suicide with a pistol in the pool when I was ten. Grief stricken and unable to continue conducting the Cleveland Philharmonic, my dad drank himself to sleep every night until his liver gave out. One morning I found him in bed, covered in bloody vomit, dead. I was their only child. And now *I'm* half dead at forty four."

The soft touch of her hands caressing my nape and the returning warmth in her voice made me want to crush her in my arms, but I pulled back and smeared her tears with my thumb. She

115

smiled and tilted her head to look directly into my eyes. "You know," I said, "much as I love engines, I can't ignore the feelings I have for you."

Having revealed more than I intended, I quickly pulled back from her embrace. "Hey, I forgot to tell you. I got the generator running. Mostly just water in the gas. It was stuck, too, but it came free when I gave the flywheels some body English."

Porter lowered her chin, turned her head a little to one side and looked at me from the corners of her eyes. "Filson, you didn't. With all the other stuff going on?"

"Had to, to power your radio to call the Coast Guard."

"No *other* reason, I suppose."

"Say, when can we get you out of here?"

"The doctor thinks I can go home Thursday, after he's sure...."

It was all I could do to hold back my tears.

This morning on the way to the truck, Witte stooped to pick up a woolly bear caterpillar. She handed it to me. "Hard winter comin'; awful hard."

I studied the hairy tiger moth larva coiled tight against the cold in my palm. It was solid black, not a trace of brown in its coat. I looked into my wife's close-set gray eyes. There, behind the reflected brilliance of an unusually colorful October morning in Maine, behind the tongues of flame licking the pines, the sky seethed a diesel brown.

"Don't tell me you believe in caterpillar forecasting," I said, letting the critter roll off my hand and fall to the ground. I opened the driver's door of our 1929 Ford AA truck, slid under the wheel and bent to open the fuel tap.

Witte said, "Bluebirds been actin' queer since spring. Didn't mate or nest at all." She hiked into the passenger seat and slammed the door. "Pattin, too. I mean it, Karcher, we're in for it."

I set the spark and throttle levers for starting but didn't crank. "What in blazes has our daughter got to do with the weather, Witte? Bluebird behavior, maybe. But Pattin?"

"She's most thirty-one. Can't keep a man."

"Perhaps she's a lesbian." I yanked the choke and trod the starter. The Ford groaned twice through compression and sputtered to life, settling into a rolling rich idle.

"Can't keep a girlfriend, either."

"Then she's probably asexual." I crunched into first and popped the clutch. The Ford lurched from the driveway and headed down Broad Turn Road for the Murch farm.

* * * * * *

Pattin had left us for Manhattan when she was seventeen, first to attend N.Y.U., then Juilliard. After college she stayed to study recorder with Lamaar Petri. Breaking into the early music business wasn't easy, but within five years she was performing with the Krainin Consort in Alice Tully Hall at Lincoln Center. Witte and I were very proud of her and gave her a Levin and Silverstein alto for Christmas. A year later she quit Krainin and started her own Renaissance group. Soon she was flying to London to play Gibbons galliards and Lasso madrigals in Wigmore Hall, then on to Israel where her Bourree Band regaled an elite Tel Aviv audience with Praetorius' *Terpsichore*. Except for brief visits, she never returned to Maine. We'd get a call from her every couple months. But the calls ceased last April, and she didn't show up at the lake this summer. Worried, Witte rang her up in September. They talked for an hour. "I'm okay, Mom…honest. You don't need to call me." I sensed that she didn't want to talk to her father.

* * * * * *

Despite disuse and infrequent servicing, the old Ford truck chuffed the five miles to my in-laws' farm without incident. Witte posted alongside me in silence, staring straight ahead, while I visually roved the autumn colors. It was one of those McIntosh days: crisp, cool and polished to a high luster, the kind of day that inspires one to work up wood for winter—just the prescription for our assigned mission.

I had rigged the truck chassis with a tilting table cordwood saw driven by a wide flat belt from Wilbur, my Fairbanks-Morse one-lunger. Witte and I began buzzing firewood for ourselves and a few of the neighbors. But the word got around, and before long we had a small but loyal clientele of woodburners within a half hour's chug from our home in Buxton who wanted our service. With its low gearing, the ton-and-a-half Ford was only good for thirty miles per hour, so we were restricted to a fifteen mile radius.

Witte's father Loring got first priority in the fall, having "engineered" the saw rig, patterning the quaint contraption after his dad's horse-drawn Economy. It was for Loring, now seventy-five, that we were to buzz wood that Saturday. He met us at the kitchen door dressed in work wool from his cap to his boots. "Good," he said. "Wheel her over to them slabs back of the barn." He waved a bony finger south. "Got five cord oak scraps from Chute's. No charge. They's tinder dry. Doak delivered 'em yesterday."

"You're lucky," I said. "Most mills charge for tailings. I know L.C. Andrews does."

Loring looked at Witte, who had made no gesture of greeting. "What's eatin' you?"

Witte's lips drew to a line. I shrugged, feigning innocence. Loring shook his head and swung aboard the right front fender. I put the Ford in low-low and crawled over the rye stubble toward the barn.

When I stopped to back up to the slab pile, Witte jumped out and began ministering to Wilbur. Her jaw remained set as her hands fluttered over the engine, tweaking the grease cups, starting the cylinder oiler and setting its drip rate. Off came the bicycle tire from the saw.

I dismounted and approached cautiously with the oil can. Ignoring my presence, Witte weakened Wilbur's compression and bent the belt onto the pulleys, climbing the spokes on the left flywheel to keep it turning. I'd never seen her so intent, so determined to upstage me.

But when she snatched the oil can from my hand and began shooting the timing gears, I had to defend myself. Ordinarily, I wouldn't air our differences in front of Loring, but Witte's takeover of Wilbur made me boiling mad. "What in hell have I done to deserve this?"

Witte shoved me aside and began letting down the jacks from under the truck frame to steady the rig when sawing. Loring kept his distance.

Jacking done, Witte moved to Wilbur's mixer and opened the needle valve a full turn. "You fill this thing with gas?" she barked, positioning the flywheels for choking. Wilbur sighed. I nodded and tried to say something arresting, but no words came out. Witte covered the choke with one hand, gripped the left flywheel at the top with the other and pushed hard. The impulse magneto snapped at top dead center. Then the check valve in the tank made a strangling noise. She pulled her hand from the choke but kept the wheels turning. When the magneto struck again, Wilbur took a weak impulse and disgorged a loud burp. "There," she said, confirming Wilbur's readiness. She looked me in the eye for the first time since we'd left Windham. "Well?"

I lunged for the right flywheel and together we pulled Wilbur over center. He hit harder this time and sent a sooty ring of smoke aloft. We sprang back. Cannonlike reports erupted from Wilbur's stack in building cadence until he fetched up against the governor, whereupon he closed his throttle and began issuing a train of swinelike snorts and grunts. The saw whispered as the belt lashed and wove between the sheaves, its lacing ticking with the regularity of a mantle clock. I glanced at Loring. He was smiling.

With all the commotion, there was no opening for me to inject an invective. Wilbur's restlessness drew all hands to work. Witte and I fell into our familiar rhythm, together picking the eight-foot slabs from the pile and loading them onto the table, I then bending the wood to the saw, Witte supporting then flinging the shorts into her dad's truck parked alongside.

Loring headed off to the barn for water. Returning with two half-full pails, he emptied one into Wilbur's hopper then leaned the mixture until the exhaust sharpened and belched pale yellow flame. Satisfied, he approached Witte and insisted on spelling her. "I'll take her awhile," he bellowed between Wilbur's blats and the saw's mournful cries.

"Five slabs, Daddy. That's all." Witte pulled off her gloves and took a seat on the nearside running board of Loring's truck, to keep a close eye on her father.

Witte's mother Ida had been dead for seven years, and Witte felt responsible for her father's wellbeing. She and Loring were as much alike in temperament as Pattin and I. With Loring and Witte, cussedness seemed to be the uniting factor, a stubborn stability that made Maine granite seem crumbly by comparison.

By contrast, Pattin and I rode emotional roller coasters, each rising from the depth of depression to a pinnacle of joy, only to break over the top and swoop down into the dark again. We'd repeat the sinusoidal pattern over and over but at different frequencies. Sometimes our mercurial paths would superimpose, and we'd lock in harmony awhile, sharing the augmented anguish and ecstasy of hearts beating in resonance. But mostly it was a mismatch. Lately we'd been missing one another more than hitting it off. And that bothered Witte a lot. It was hard for so centered a woman to witness our desultory behavior.

"That's enough," Witte shouted, tugging at Loring's sleeve. "Give it a rest."

Loring looked crestfallen. He jammed his hands deep into his pockets and walked slowly toward the house. It was the first time I'd seen him give in to Witte's will. Age has a way of draining the sap from a man.

* * * * * *

Clarence came by with the mail at noon on Saturday. When we were home, Witte would usually meet him at the corner to catch up on the latest gossip. This Saturday we didn't get back until nearly dark because of the size of the woodpile and Loring's lecturing us for almost an hour over lunch. We stopped at the letterbox on the way in. Along with the mail-order catalogs and bills, there was a letter from Pattin, the first we'd received in almost a year. Witte tore open the envelope with trembling fingers. As she read in silence, the color drained from her face and her small mouth puckered until it resembled a grape lifesaver.

"What is it, Witte? What'd she say?"

Witte handed me the letter. She slumped against the door and exhaled a full breath.

I looked at the single sheet of recycled paper printed with shamrocks. Neatly lettered in Pattin's round hand was a brief note addressed, "Dear Karcher and Witte."

I put the paper down. "Oh, boy. Not Taddos and Momby. Not even Dad and Mom, but Karcher and Witte. And it's dated, simply, October 1992. No day, just the month." I picked up the letter again and began reading:

> *I have recently become aware of events from my childhood which I need time to work out without interacting with you or anyone in the family. I am not able to discuss this, nor answer questions. I don't know how long it will take, and only I will know when it's time for me to return from this separation.*
>
> *I will not be joining you for birthdays, Thanksgiving or Christmas. I do not want to exchange gifts or cards. Please do not call me or write to me unless there is a life-threatening accident or death in the immediate family. This includes Grandpa. I will let you explain it to him as you see fit. I need to be completely out of contact while I work things out.*
>
> *I will contact you when I am ready. Please respect my wishes and trust that I am doing what is best to take care of myself.*
> *Pattin*

"I always knew she was a feisty kid," I said, "but this takes it. She's got a lot of Moxie dropping out for the holidays. I bet her therapist put her up to this; probably told her what to write. God damn her—both of them. I'll tell you, Witte, she's not going to waltz back in here next spring or summer and jump into her daddy's waiting arms.

"Remember how I used to tell you that she didn't want to talk to me when you'd ask me to phone her? I had a feeling she was angry with us, with me especially."

"I need some air, deah." Witte let herself out of the truck and began walking slowly toward the house, much the way her father had done earlier in the day.

Fears of Pattin, unable to tell us she'd contracted AIDS or had swapped sexual preference, flitted across my mind like bats hunting over a pond at dusk. I brushed them aside on my way to the kitchen, remembering Pattin's emotional pattern and the last episode she had pulled on us. Witte was preparing supper when I came in.

"You know," I said, "this has happened before, though not as dramatically. Remember two years ago, also in October, when she suddenly flew up to see us after months of being sullen and reclusive?"

"Yuh." Witte's acknowledgement was barely audible, formed as she drew a quick, shallow breath.

"She was so loving and apologetic and took a long walk with me to relate her painful childhood memories in a way that I wouldn't get upset. She was so grown up and considerate. It was the first time she'd confronted me with her problems. I was touched that she'd felt able to tell me about the conflict. We were so proud of her progress in therapy. Remember?"

"Yuh," Witte inhaled.

"Well, it's happening again. Something must have triggered her."

"It's Bruce. She lost him, deah."

"Bruce? The gay architect she's been friends with for years?" Witte nodded.

"That's too bad. He was a good buddy. What happened?"

Witte put down the pot in her hand and approached me. "Karcher, there's somethin' I haven't told you. Sit down." I braced myself on the back of a chair but didn't sit.

"Pattin confided last Christmas that she was goin' with Bruce. Sexually, I mean."

"Oh, sure. Uh-huh. And I suppose he just snapped straight after living with Bill for twelve years."

"It didn't happen that fast, deah. Pattin said he'd started havin' feelings for her that summer. He kep' it to himself till he was sure. They've been datin' now for almost a year."

"Jeezus. This is worse than I imagined. What are we to do?"

123

"Nothin', like she said."

"What about Loring? How are we going to tell him? He'll be broken. You know how he loves that girl."

"*We* aren't. *I* am."

"Good. And do it when I'm not around, please." I sank to a seat, bent over the kitchen table and buried my face in my hands.

Witte sat down beside me and began stroking the back of my head like she used to do when I'd get a panic attack and start hyperventilating to quell my nausea. "Pattin's just reactin' to you like you reacted to your mother, deah. All those times she got crazy and had to be given a shot of Thorazine by the doctor next door. When Pattin was little and you had a spell, I'd have to get you the fan and phenobarbital, put you to bed with the radio on, later bring you tea and dry toast—she saw all that. She'd ask, 'What's wrong with Daddy?' I'd tell her not to worry, that you'd be okay in the mornin'. She'd give me this look like she didn't believe me and run to her room and lock the door."

I sat up and pounded the table with my fist. "She's goddamn lucky I never laid a hand on her or made sexual advances like so many fathers do. Hell, I never even saw her naked past age seven."

"No, you was a gentleman, always, deah." Witte took my hand between hers. "It's just that she's very sensitive, Karcher. She was confused. One minute you was her father, next you was a sick child.

"It's my fault, too. When I pretended nothin' was wrong, she could see I was lyin'. She felt I had to fix you, like she had to be the mother, 'cause she figured I wasn't takin' you bein' sick seriously."

"So, she had no childhood, either. Oh, God, I didn't want her to have to live *my* legacy."

Witte bent over me and whispered, "Karcher, Karcher, it's not so bad as you say. You was a good father, and strong so much of the time. She just took it very hard."

"I feel so helpless. There's nothing I can do to erase what happened. And now she's left us. I might as well be dead, like Nettie."

"Now, stop. Your mother was very sick. You're much better off. You don't drink. You're only attracted to women. You got professional help. And you're still alive. Gosh, you hardly ever have a spell anymore."

"Yeah. Now, I just feel crappy. I feel worthless—a failure as a father."

"Look, it's Pattin's problem now, not yours or mine. She's gotta get herself out of it. Best we leave her alone. She'll come back."

"I'm not so sure this time."

Witte sighed. "Truth is, I'm not, either, deah."

Man made to make Man happy
A music engine that made him sad
With waterfalls and painted moonlight
And children shouting to be free
All folded up inside.

It churned and struggled to be heard
Over the din of Man's living
Yet Man rejected it
For the insistent voice he gave it.
He scratched its face and covered its mouth
And when it refused to be quiet
He turned its face to the wall
And pulled the plug.

Some listened and decried the silence
They brushed away its cobweb tears
Patched its leather, oiled its gears
But as if its life arrested
Its childlike voice had not matured
And they were happy being sad
Hearing songs of yesteryears.

In the cobwebbed world of mechanical music, the unique voice of the Wurlitzer band organ has attracted a small but loyal following but repelled the majority of pneumatic fanatics. Some of its critics are moved most by the mechanical instrument that comes closest to playing and sounding like a human performer, a combo, or an orchestra. To them, the Wurlitzer organ is a musical disgrace because it sounds mechanical. They find its limited musical capabilities frustrating. Others dislike its uneven voicing and loud tone and are disgusted by the repetition of its arrangements. Let's face it: it's not very musical in the classical sense, even for a band organ.

What makes this Model T of organs so moving to some of us? We expect a mechanical instrument to act and sound mechanical and are disappointed if it performs humanly. Most band organs exude a mechanical flavor, but none can match the martial precision of a Wurlitzer with its prompt action, quick pipe speech, and abrupt musical arrangements.

Sadly, most Wurlitzer organs found today, if playing at all, are wheezing ghosts of their former selves. We might be lucky enough to catch a hint of their snappy melodies amid the stumbling, flapping, and caterwauling of a carnival-owned sample. But to capture the essence of the Wurlitzer band organ sound, as with any pneumatic instrument, requires an organ in top condition. Add a properly arranged music roll and the punctual, drilling trills, crisp bell glissandos, and crackling snare-drum rolls pour forth unfettered.

Many of the Wurlitzer arrangements took advantage of the instrument's mechanical promptness and called for intricate, syncopated snare-drum rhythms, grace notes and rapid note repetition. Marches played on a Wurlitzer take on a special urgency, a driving and exciting vitality not experienced with other fairground instruments. A Wurlitzer, in fact, never stops marching. Fox-trots, waltzes, one-steps, and polkas all get belted out in a militaristic style—but with a special twist of melancholy.

Perhaps most distinctive of all is the Wurlitzer military band organ tone, and it is especially this factor that has been responsible for our devotion to the instrument. Its wooden (holz) trumpets have an afternoon sound that blends with the setting sun: pungent, haunting, sometimes sinister—never cheerful. These trumpet voices are mournful. They bloom and have silvery edges. The sound of a Wurlitzer band organ is more capable of inducing a flood of tears than any instrument I know. And yet, with all its melancholy, it manages to sound unbreakable, dependable, and everlasting.

A Wurlitzer band organ is a sincere instrument with never a trace of frivolity in its voice. It works hard at making music and lets you know it. Sometimes it's almost painful to listen to its childlike struggling—all the earnest huffing and puffing, the missing sharps, the relentless crashing of its traps, the simplistic oompah of its abbreviated bass scale. It seems at times like a St. Bernard puppy innocently flattening all the flowers in the garden, so hard does it try to please.

But there's a message in its song, strength in its dependable marching—strength to work for hours without rest, strength to carry on when neglected or mistreated. To some of us, it imparts that same strength.

Robert

The month was May, and oh so fair
We cranked the organ on the square
For throngs of folk who needed air
And Robert saw us standing there

He moved our way with twisted smile
On wobbly legs, his breath was vile
Grasped the lion, once plush with pile
And danced for us, did he beguile

With stammer and slur, his one request
"Teach me, please, to play the best"
I winced as he put me to the test
"Next year," I said at his behest

He stayed with us the whole day long
We walked. The lion? It came along
He drank but milk, his flask was gone
Then slept, the chair to him did not belong

We took his picture and offered one
His address we asked, but there was none
He said a subway pillow is no fun
You see, poor Robert was a bum

Greenwich Village, 5/22/86

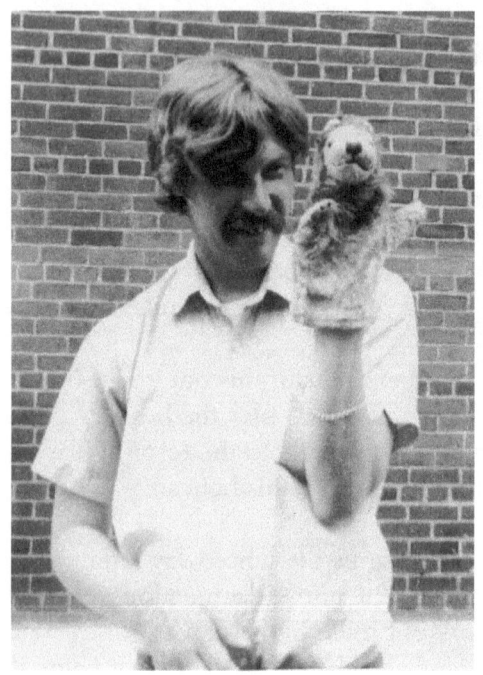

Robert

It happened again on Sunday, but this time I wasn't soaped up when the shower quit. I hadn't been under the water more than a minute before the spray dwindled to a trickle, then a drip. What could it be *this* time?

I'll bet the pump line froze up, my comeuppance for switching off the in-pipe heater to save electricity. But it's barely below freezing, and Sebago Lake never iced up the whole winter.

Muttering, I dried and dressed. After breakfast and a heated discussion with my wife about the insanity of retiring on a lake in Maine, I headed out to uncover the underground pump house. To free the hatch, I had to chip away several inches of opaque ice and stomp on the cover until I could pry it up.

The centrifugal pump was chortling away in its subterranean sauna, but its pressure gauge was twitching zero. For a moment I contemplated trying to prime the pump, but there was no ladder to descend to its level, so I switched it off and turned on the pipe heater. Then we waited.

Three hours later I tried the pump again. Still no water.

It was about noon when I called our plumber Doak. A young boy answered. From his speech pattern, I figured the kid couldn't have been much over two years old. "Heh-woe."

"Is your daddy there?"

Scuffling noises erupted, and then a clunk, as if the tyke had dropped the phone. I waited.

"Heh-woe. Who's zis?"

"Hi. Listen, is your father at home—the plumber?"

More scuffling sounds. Then the little voice said, "What's goin' on?"

"Excuse me?"

"What's goin' on?" the kid said, louder this time.

"Well, let's see. We're out of water here, and look, may I speak to the plumber, please?"

Apparently my declaration of distress had satisfied the boy, for the next voice I heard was deep and resonant.

"What's goin' on?"

"Oh. Hi, Doak. Sorry to bother you on a Sunday, but we're without water—again."

"What's goin' on?"

"Well, the pump's running, but it seems to be cavitating."

"What's goin' on?"

"I don't know, Doak. That's why I'm calling you."

I paused. When Doak didn't say anything, I continued, "We're really in a jam here. When can you come over?"

"Today?"

"Yes. Look here, Doak. This lake water system has never been right from the day you installed it."

"Zat so?"

Oh boy. As soon as I heard 'Zat so,' I knew I'd lost my leverage. When a Mainer says 'Zat so,' he's locked up. Nothing more can get through. But I was too angry to let the matter drop.

"I want it fixed once and for all this time, Doak."

"Zat so?"

I was going to blow; I knew it. My wife knew it too from my color. "Draw a deep breath," she whispered. I did, and Doak must have heard my gasp.

"How long you gonna be there?" he asked.

"Well, we have to go out at four. Could you make it before then?"

"I'd like to, I really would. But Evie just came home from the hospital, and I've gotta stay close."

"Oh, sure. I understand. Hey, next week would be fine. We can flush with buckets from the lake till you get here."

"I'll be there Tuesday—or Wednesday—end of the week for sure."

"I don't think it's anything serious," I said.

"Prolly suckin' air again, is all."

"There. Sounds like you've figured it out already. Thanks, Doak, and sorry to catch you at a bad time. Listen, best to Evie. Hope she mends fast. See you next week. B--bye."

When I hung up, my wife said, "I told you we should have hired that outfit in Portland instead of a local bozo."

"Oh, Doak's all right. He's just afraid to tighten the fittings enough."

"That's what I mean. He's incompetent. Remember the flood he caused under the bathroom sink?"

"You mean, when he left the supply pipe nuts loose?"

"Yes, and I had to mop up half the lake downstairs."

"Doak's got to learn somehow."

"Here? At our expense?"

"They call it 'on-the-job training'."

"Zat so?" my wife replied.

About the Author

Kevin Sheehan is a retired mechanical engineer who first fell in love with Maine at age two, in 1939, imprinted by a steam locomotive at Portland Union Station. He studied at Cornell and graduated New York University in 1960. For thirty-three years, he tested and reported on cars for Consumers Union, publisher of *Consumer Reports*. His short articles and poetry have appeared in *Down East*, *Out of the Cradle*, *WoodenBoat*, and the *Bulletin* of the Musical Box Society International. His first novel, *The Aberration*, was published in 2012 by North Country Press. Kevin and his wife Lindy share a lakeside log cabin in Sebago, Maine.

www.ingramcontent.com/pod-product-compliance
Lightning Source LLC
Chambersburg PA
CBHW052146170626
46812CB00004B/1614